The Leader in You

The Leader in You

Dale Carmegie

PRABHAT
PRAKASHAN

Published by
PRABHAT PRAKASHAN PVT. LTD.
4/19 Asaf Ali Road,
New Delhi-110 002 (INDIA)
e-mail: prabhatbooks@gmail.com

ISBN 978-93-5266-493-1
THE LEADER IN YOU
by Dale Carnegie

Edition
Second, 2025

Typesetting
Team Prabhat

Paperback Price
₹ 450.00 (Rupees Four Hundred Fifty only)

Printed at
R-Tech Offset Printers, Delhi

INTRODUCTION
The Human-Relations Revolution

Keep your mind open to change all the time. Welcome it. Court it. It is only by examining and reexamining your opinions and ideas that you can progress.

—DALE CARNEGIE

As the twenty-first century approaches, the world is undergoing enormous change, a process of great upheaval and great possibility. In just a few short years, we have witnessed the dawn of postindustrial society, the advent of the information age, the rush to computerization, the birth of biotechnology, and not the least of these changes, the human-relations revolution.

With the end of the cold war, the business environment has grown dramatically more intense. Competition has become more global and more energized. And technology races on. No longer can businesses safely ignore their customers' wants and needs. No longer can managers simply issue orders and expect them to be mindlessly obeyed. No longer can personal relationships be taken for granted. No longer can companies be less than obsessed with constant quality improvement. No longer can so much human creativity go so scandalously untapped.

To survive in the years to come, successful organizations—in business, in government, in the nonprofit World —will have to undergo a profound cultural change.

Their people will have to think quicker, work smarter, dream wilder, and relate to each other in very different ways.

Most important of all, this cultural change will require a whole new breed of leader, a leader quite unlike the bosses most of us have worked for and some of us have perhaps become. The day has long since passed when a company could be run with a bullwhip and a chair.

The leaders of tomorrow will have to establish a real vision and a sense of values for the organizations they wish to lead. These leaders will have to communicate and motivate far more effectively than did leaders of the past. They will have to keep their wits about them through conditions of near-constant change. And these new leaders will have to mine every ounce of talent and creativity that their organizations possess —from the shop floor to the executive suite.

The roots of all this upheaval can be traced back to the decades that followed World War II. In the postwar years American companies seemed to prosper almost regardless of what they did. The economies of Europe and Asia were hobbled by the war's destruction, and the world's developing countries were not much of an economic factor yet. Big American-based companies, backed by big labor and big government, set the standards for everyone else. It wasn't that these companies were so beautifully run. They never really had to be. With their steep hierarchies, their rigid job descriptions, and their we-know-best attitudes, they cruised right through the middle years of the century —fat, happy, and as profitable as could be.

What lovely cocoons these companies provided for their employees! A job with a decent corporation was for many people a job for life—not so different from the civil service, but with a better salary and sweeter fringe benefits.

Layoffs? Who ever heard of layoffs for people who wore suit jackets or dresses to work? Maybe for factory workers, but definitely not for the managerial set. People spoke often about "the ladder of success," and that's how they would progress in their careers, one rung at a time, neither slower nor faster than the people above or below. In hindsight we see that those were the days of easy affluence; eventually they had to end.

While America was enjoying the fruits of the postwar era, the Japanese were thinking ahead. Their economy was destroyed, much of their basic infrastructure was in ruins, and that was just the beginning of what the Japanese had to overcome. They also had a worldwide reputation for producing cheap, shoddy goods and delivering second-rate customer service.

But after all the hardship they had suffered, the Japanese were ready to learn from their mistakes. So they went out and hired the best advisors they could find, among them Dr. W. Edwards Deming, a statistician who had worked in the United States Army's quality control office during the war.

Deming's message to the Japanese: Don't try to copy the intricate structures of big American corporations. Instead, Deming and others advised, build a new kind of Japanese company—a company dedicated to employee involvement, quality improvement, and customer satisfaction—and work to unite all the employees behind those goals.

It didn't happen overnight, but the Japanese economy was reborn. Japan became a leader in technological innovation, and the quality of Japanese goods and services soared. With this new spirit in place, Japanese firms didn't just catch up with their foreign competitors. In many important industries, the Japanese rolled right past. It didn't take long for their approach to begin spreading around the globe—to Germany, to Scandinavia, across the Far East, and along the Pacific Rim. America, unfortunately, was one of the last to catch on. This delay proved costly.

Slowly, imperceptibly at first, America's cruise of easy affluence was running out of gas. Through the 1960s and the 1970s, the roar of the postwar economy was loud enough to drown out the occasional sputters, but the hints of trouble grew increasingly hard to ignore. Oil got expensive. Inflation and interest rates shot up. And competition wasn't coming only from a reinvigorated Japan or Germany anymore. Dozens of other countries overseas, little blips on the economic landscape, suddenly arrived at the cutting edge of technology with newly sharpened competitive skills. Before long they too were capturing major market shares from General Motors, from Zenith, from IBM, from Kodak, and from other slumbering corporate giants.

By the mid-1980s the growing trouble was becoming difficult to contain. Real estate took a tumble. Corporate debt and the national deficit ballooned. The stock market started doing peculiar things. The nagging recession that settled over the early 1990s showed once and for all how different the world had grown.

For the people caught in the middle, all this change seemed to arrive at white-knuckle speed. If companies weren't undergoing a corporate merger or acquisition, they were restructuring or taking a dip in the chilly waters of bankruptcy court. There were firings. There were layoffs. The change was brutal. It was swift. And it wasn't just blue-collar anymore. Professionals and executives all across the white-collar ranks were coming face to face with a narrowing future, and they were not quite sure what to do.

Predictably, change of this magnitude and speed has very much affected how people feel about themselves and their careers. From one end of the economy to the other, it has produced unprecedented waves of dissatisfaction and fear.

Some people have placed their faith in technology, figuring the world can simply invent its way out of this current state of affairs. And there's no denying the contribution that technology can make.

"I can walk into my office in New York and use the exact same data that someone in Japan is using—at exactly the same moment," says Thomas A. Saunders III, general partner at Saunders Karp & Company, a private merchant bank. "We're connected to the same data system, twenty-four hours a day. People everywhere in the world are hardwired together in a communications network that is far more sophisticated than anyone envisioned. Capital markets and currency markets are beyond government control. And I don't need a newspaper to tell me anything about any of those markets."

"What you see are the profits of evolution at work, increasing the potential so that more can be done in a shorter period of time," says Dr. Jonas Salk, medicine's great researcher. "We've got more people collaborating at greater distances, so at this point more is possible in a shorter period of time than a hundred years ago. The more resources you have, the more means you have to progress."

"Remember when computers first appeared?" asks Malcolm S. Forbes, Jr., editor-in-chief of the business magazine that bears his family's name. "They were feared instruments of Big Brother. Television was feared to be an instrument of propaganda. But thanks to high technology, they've had the opposite effect. The computer became smaller and much less of a mainframe. Power grew astronomically, so you weren't tied down anymore.

"The microchip is extending the reach of the human brain the way machines extended the reach of the human muscle in the last century. Today software is becoming the slabs of steel. Fiber optics and digital screens are becoming the railroads and the highways for transportation, and so information is raw material."

"Now," Forbes goes on, "you can do your messaging and your computer work on a little, two-pounder on your lap —and do it anywhere you can find a plug or a satellite." The result? More people have more access to more information. "People can see what's happening in the rest of the world," Forbes concludes. "It's a very democratizing influence."

The fall of the Berlin Wall, the disintegration of the Sovietbloc, the uprisings in China, the struggles for democracy in Latin America and the Caribbean, the ongoing industrialization of the developing world— all these changes signal a new industrial freedom and a new recognition that the world is a community. Every one of these changes has been pushed along by wider access to communication technology.

Striking images of this change are now routinely beamed around the world. Chinese students wave English-language banners for the cameras. Saddam Hussein—and for that matter, the American Joint Chiefs of Staff—both followed the progress of the Persian Gulf War on CNN.

But technology alone is never enough in difficult times. Just because the means of communication are readily available doesn't mean that people have learned to communicate well. Far too often today, they haven't. This is one of the ironies of modern times: the great capacity to communicate, the great failure to do so. What good is all this information if people don't know how to share it?

Not long ago the Graduate School of Business at Harvard University conducted a survey of its students, alumni, and recruiters. Given the pressing need for communication today, the results should come as no surprise. "What we are finding," says Harvard business school professor John A. Quelch, "is a large measure of satisfaction with the technical competence of the graduating students."

These bright young people can crunch numbers, analyze markets, and devise business plans, but when it comes to teaching human-relations skills, Harvard is stepping up its efforts. "That seems to be the area where improvements are needed," Quelch observes. "Oral and written communication, teamwork, and other human skills."

Yet those are exactly the skills that will go farthest in determining the success of these young business leaders.

Sure, technological sophistication will still be important as the world races ahead, but that is just the price of admission to the new business arena. In the end the winners and losers will not be divided by their bytes and RAMs. The winners will be the organizations with smart and creative leaders who know how to communicate and motivate effectively—inside the organization and out.

"Good human-relations skills have the ability to change people from managing others to leading others," says John Rampey, director of management development at Milliken & Company, a leading textile manufacturer. People can learn to move "from directing to guiding, from competing to collaborating, from operating under a system of veiled secrecy to one of sharing information as it's needed, from a mode of passivity to a mode of risk taking, from one of viewing people as an expense to one of viewing people as an asset." They can learn how "to change lives from resentment to contentment, from apathy to involvement, from failure to success."

No one ever said these skills would come naturally, and frequently they do not. "It isn't that easy to know how to provide superior human relationships," says Burt Manning, chairman of J. Walter Thompson Company, the worldwide advertising firm. "There are a few people who do it instinctively. But most people have to be educated. They have to be trained. It takes as much training—and as much sophistication—as it does to be an engineer in a car company and to design a better piston.

"Those companies that can create a cadre of human beings who act in a way that advances the company's cause are going to beat the other guy," Manning says. "Those are the companies that understand that service and human relationships are going to be a huge differentiator in success."

Dale Carnegie didn't live long enough to see the days of easy affluence give way to the days of explosive change. And he never witnessed the arrival of this new human-relations revolution. But long before anyone had ever heard the terms corporate vision, employee empowerment, or quality-improvement process, Carnegie was pioneering some fundamental human-relations concepts that lie at the center of those important ideas.

Carnegie arrived in New York City in 1912, a young man from northwest Missouri trying to figure out what to do with his life. He eventually landed a job at the 125th Street YMCA, teaching public speaking to adults at night.

"At first," Carnegie wrote many years later, "I conducted courses in public speaking only—courses designed to train adults, by actual experience, to think on their feet and express their ideas with more clarity, more effectiveness, and more poise, both in business interviews and before groups.

"But gradually, as the seasons passed, I realized that as sorely as these adults needed training in effective speaking, they needed still more training in the fine art of getting along with people in everyday business and social contacts."

So Carnegie broadened his course to include some basic human-relations skills. He had no textbook, no official syllabus, no published course guide. But he had built a growing list of practical techniques for getting along in the world, and he was testing those techniques every day.

"Look at things from the other person's perspective," he told his students. "Give honest and sincere appreciation.

Become genuinely interested in others." He showed his students how to weave these basic human-relations principles into the fabric of their lives.

In the beginning, Carnegie just scribbled his rules on three-by-five-inch cards. Soon those cards were replaced by a leaflet, which was replaced by a series of booklets, each one larger than the last. After fifteen years of painstaking experimentation, Carnegie gathered up all his human-relations principles and put them in a book. How to Win Friends and Influence People, which appeared in 1936, was Dale Carnegie's straightforward guide to dealing successfully with others.

The book took off. Thirty million copies later, How to Win Friends was one of the best-selling books in the history of the written word. It has been translated into several dozen languages, and it is still selling today.

Carnegie formed a company, Dale Carnegie & Associates, Inc., to spread his human-relations message, and he found an eager audience around the world. He appeared regularly on radio and television. He taught others how to teach his course, and he wrote two more human-relations books, The Quick and Easy Way to Effective Speaking and How to Stop Worrying and Start Living, best sellers both. Even Carnegie's death in 1955 did not impede the spread of his ideas.

Today the Dale Carnegie Course is offered in more than a thousand cities and towns across America and in seventy other countries. Each week another three thousand people enroll. The Carnegie organization has now grown to the point that it custom designs training programs for more than four hundred of the Fortune 500 firms.

With each new generation, the Carnegie message has shown an uncanny ability to redefine itself to meet the needs of a changing world. Communicating effectively with other people, motivating them to achieve, discovering the leader inside everyone—these were the primary focus of Dale Carnegie's insight. With the world in its current state of turmoil, his time has again arrived. In the pages that follow, Carnegie's human-relations principles are applied to the unique set of challenges people face today.

These principles are basic and easy to understand. They demand no special education or technical skill. What they require is practice and a genuine willingness to learn.

Are you prepared to challenge some long-standing views of the world? Are you ready to manage your relationships with greater ease and success? Would you like to increase the value of your most precious possession, the people in your personal and professional life? Are you willing to find and release the leader in you?

If so, read on. What comes next might just change your life.

□

Editor's Note

Great leaders are individuals who are passionate about and confident in the work they do, and they inspire others to do so in the process. Dale Carnegie's vision extends from corporate team building, to improving the leadership qualities within each individual. Being it on a professional or a personal level, Dale Carnegie has been a great source of inspiration and guide strengthening all with a positive approach towards self-assessment of taking command on one's life. He has been extremely successful in igniting enthusiasm in people's views and vision towards their professional and personal lives.

By bringing out this edition of the book for our readers, we have ensured Dale Carnegie's approach is well-directed to the reader with sheer precision, as the way author would have wanted to be presented.

The Leader in You is an expressive step-by-step guide; demonstrating tips, ideas, and strategies on principles to have an creative and exciting work life, irrespective of in what profession one is.

□

Editor's Note

Contents

Chapter—1

Finding the Leader in You

Charles Schwab was paid a salary of a million dollars a year in the steel business, and he told me that he was paid this huge salary largely because of his ability to handle people. Imagine that! A million dollars a year because he was able to handle people! One day at noontime, Schwab was walking through one of his steel mills when he came across a group of men smoking directly under a sign that said No Smoking.

Do you suppose that Charles Schwab pointed at the sign and said, "Can't you read?"

Absolutely not, not that master of human relations.

Mr. Schwab chatted with the men in a friendly way and never said a word about the fact that they were smoking under a No Smoking sign.

Finally he handed them some cigars and said with a twinkle in his eye, "I'd appreciate it, boys, if you'd smoke these outside."

That is all he said. Those men knew that he knew that they had broken a rule, and they admired him because he hadn't called them down. He had been such a good sport with them that they in turn wanted to be good sports with him.

—DALE CARNEGIE

Fred Wilpon is the president of the New York Mets baseball team. One afternoon Wilpon was leading a group of school children on a tour of Shea Stadium. He let them stand behind home plate. He took them into the team dugouts. He walked them through the private passage to the clubhouse. As the final stop on his tour, Wilpon wanted to take the students into the stadium bull pen, where the pitchers warm up.

But right outside the bull pen gate, the group was stopped by a uniformed security guard.

"The bull pen isn't open to the public," the guard told Wilpon, obviously unaware of who he was. "I'm sorry, but you can't go out there."

Now, Fred Wilpon certainly had the power to get what he wanted right then and there. He could have berated the poor security guard for failing to recognize such an important person as himself. With a dramatic flourish, Wilpon could have whipped out his top-level security pass and shown the wide-eyed children how much weight he carried at Shea.

Wilpon did none of that. He led the students to the far side of the stadium and took them into the bull pen through another gate.

Why did he bother to do that? Wilpon didn't want to embarrass the security guard. The man, after all, was doing his job and doing it well. Later that afternoon Wilpon even sent off a handwritten note, thanking the guard for showing such concern.

Had Wilpon chosen instead to yell or cause a scene, the guard might well have ended up feeling resentful, and no doubt his work would have suffered as a result. Wilpon's gentle approach made infinitely more sense. The guard feltgreat about the compliment. And you can bet he'll recognize Wilpon the next time the two of them happen to meet.

Fred Wilpon is a leader and not just because of the title he holds or the salary he earns. What makes him a leader of men and women is how he has learned to interact.

In the past people in the business world didn't give much thought to the true meaning of leadership. The boss was the boss, and he was in charge. Period. End of discussion.

Well-run companies—no one ever spoke about "well-led companies"—were the ones that operated in almost military style. Orders were delivered from above and passed down through the ranks.

Remember Mr. Dithers from the Blondie comic strip? "BUM-STEAD!" he would scream, and young Dagwood would come rushing into the boss's office like a frightened puppy. Lots of real-life companies operated that way for years. The companies that weren't run like army platoons were barely run at all. They just puttered along as they always had, secure in some little niche of a market that hadn't been challenged for years. The message from above was always, "If it ain't broke, why fix it?"

The people who had responsibility sat in their offices and managed what they could. That's what they were expected to do —to "manage." Maybe they steered the organizations a few degrees to the left or a few degrees to the right. Usually they tried to deal with whatever obvious problems presented themselves, and then they called it a day.

Back when the world was a simpler place, management like this was fine. Rarely visionary, but fine, as life rolled predictably along.

But mere management simply isn't enough anymore. The world is too unpredictable, too volatile, too fast-moving for such an uninspired approach. What's needed now is something much deeper than old-fashioned business management. What's needed is leadership, to help people achieve what they are capable of, to establish a vision for the future, to encourage, to coach and to mentor, and to establish and maintain successful relationships.

"Back when business operated in a more stable environment, management skills were sufficient," says Harvard business school professor John Quelch. "But when the business environment becomes volatile, when the waters are uncharted, when your mission requires greater flexibility than you ever imagined it would—that's when leadership skills become critical."

"The change is already taking place, and I'm not sure all organizations are ready for it," says Bill Makahilahila, Director of Human Resources at SGS-Thomson Microelectronics, Inc., a leading semiconductor manufacturer. "The position called 'manager' may not exist too much longer, and the concept of 'leadership' will be redefined. Companies today are going through that struggle. They are realizing, as they begin to downsize their operations and reach for greater productivity, that facilitative skills are going to be primary. Good communication, interpersonal skills, the ability to coach, model, and build teams—all of that requires more and better leaders.

"You can't do it by directive anymore. It has to be by influence. It takes real 'people skills.'"

Many people still have a narrow understanding of what leadership really is. You say, "leader" and they think general, president, prime minister, or chairman of the board. Obviously, people in those exalted positions are expected to lead, an expectation they meet with varying levels of success. But the fact of the matter is that leadership does not begin and end at the very top. It is every bit as important, perhaps more important, in the places most of us live and work.

Organizing a small work team, energizing an office support staff, keeping things happy at home—those are the front lines of leadership. Leadership is never easy. But thankfully, something else is also true: Every one of us has the potential to be a leader every day.

The team facilitator, the middle manager, the account executive, the customer-service operator, the person who works in the mail room—just about anyone who ever comes in contact with others has good reason to learn how to lead.

To an enormous degree their leadership skills will determine how much success they achieve and how happy they will be. Not just at work, either. Families, charity groups, sports teams, civic associations, social clubs, you name it—every one of those organizations has a tremendous need for dynamic leadership.

Steven Jobs and Steven Wozniak were a couple of blue-jeans-wearing kids from California, ages twenty-one and twenty-six. They weren't rich, they had absolutely no business training, and they were hoping to get started in an industry that barely existed at the time.

The year was 1976, before most people ever thought about buying computers for their homes. In those days the entire home-computer business added up to just a few brainy hobbyists, the original "computer nerds." So when Jobs and Wozniak scraped together thirteen hundred dollars by selling a van and two calculators and opened Apple Computer, Inc., in Job's garage, the odds against their smashing success seemed awfully long.

But these two young entrepreneurs had a vision, a clear idea of what they believed they could achieve. "Computers aren't just for nerds anymore," they announced. "Computers are going to be the bicycle of the mind. Low-cost computers are for everyone."

From day one the Apple founders kept their vision intact, and they communicated it at every turn. They hired people who understood the vision and let them share in its rewards. They lived and breathed and talked the vision. Even when the company got stalled—when the retailers said no thank you, when the manufacturing people said no way, when the bankers said no more—Apple's visionary leaders never backed down.

Eventually the world came around. Six years after Apple's founding, the company was selling 650,000 personal computers a year. Wozniak and Jobs were dynamic personal leaders, years ahead of their time.

It's not just new organizations, however, that need visionary leadership. In the early 1980s, Corning, Incorporated, was caught in a terrible squeeze. The Corning name still meant something in kitchenware, but that name was being seriously undermined. The company's manufacturing technology was outmoded. Its market share was down. Corning customers were defecting by the thousands to foreign firms. And the company's stodgy management didn't seem to have a clue.

That's when Chairman James R. Houghton concluded that Corning needed a whole new vision, and he proposed one. Recalls Houghton: "We had an outside consultant who was working with me and my new team as our resident shrink. He was really a facilitator, a wonderful guy who kept hammering on the quality issue as something we had to get into.

"We were in one of those terrible group meetings, and everybody was very depressed. I got up and announced that we were going to spend about ten million bucks that we didn't have. We were going to set up our own quality institute. We were going to get going on this.

"There were a lot of different things that put me over the top. But I am fast to admit, I just had a gut feeling that it was right. I had no idea of the implications, none, and how important it would be."

Houghton knew that Corning had to improve the quality

of its manufacturing and had to speed up delivery time. What the chairman did was take a risk. He sought advice from the best experts in the world— his own employees. Not just the manager and the company engineers. Houghton brought in the line employees too. He put a representative team together and told them to redesign Coming's entire manufacturing process —if that's what it took to bring the company around.

On the assembly line and make the machines faster to retool. The teams also reorganized the way Corning kept its inventories to get faster turnaround. The results were astounding. When Houghton launched these changes, irregularities in a new fiber-optics coating process were running eight hundred parts per million. Four years later that measure fell to zero. In two more years delivery time was cut from weeks to days, and in the space of four years Coming's return on equity nearly doubled. Houghton's vision had literally turned the company around.

Business theorists Warren Bennis and Burt Nanus have studied hundreds of successful organizations, large and small, focusing on the way in which they are led. "A leader," the two men write, "must first have developed a mental image of a possible and desirable future state of the organization. This image, which we call a vision, may be as vague as a dream or as precise as a goal or a mission statement." The critical point, Bennis and Nanus explain, "is that a vision articulates a view of a realistic, credible, attractive future for the organization, a condition that is better in some important ways than what now exists."

Leaders ask: Where is this work team heading? What does this division stand for? Who are we trying to serve? How can we improve the quality of our work? The specific answers will be as different as the people being led, as different as the leaders themselves. What's most important is that the questions are asked.

There is no one correct way to lead, and talented leaders come in many personality types. They are loud or quiet, funny or severe, tough or gentle, boisterous or shy. They come from all ages, any race, both sexes, and every kind of group there is.

The idea isn't just to identify the most successful leader you can find and then slavishly model yourself after him or her. That strategy is doomed from the start. You are unlikely ever to rise above a poor imitation of the person you are pretending to be. The leadership techniques that will work best for you are the ones you nurture inside.

Fred Ebb is a Tony Award-winning composer whose hit Broadway shows include Cabaret, Kiss of the Spider Woman, Chicago, and Zorba. Frequently, young songwriters come to Ebb for professional guidance. "I always tell them to follow the advice that Irving Berlin had for George Gershwin," Ebb says.

It seems that when Berlin and Gershwin first met, Berlin was already famous and Gershwin was just a struggling young composer working on Tin Pan Alley for thirty-five dollars a week. Impressed by Gershwin's obvious talent, Berlin offered the young man a job as his musical secretary at almost triple what Gershwin was earning writing songs.

"But don't take the job," Berlin advised. "If you do, you may develop into a second-rate Berlin. But if you insist on being yourself, someday you will become a first-rate Gershwin."

Gershwin stuck with Gershwin, of course, and American popular music reached new heights. "Don't try to imitate others," Ebb tells his proteges. "Never stop being yourself."

Often what this requires is figuring out who you really are and putting that insight thoughtfully to work. This is so important it's worth a bit of quiet reflection. Ask yourself the question in a straightforward way: What personal qualities do I possess that can be turned into the qualities of leadership?

For Robert L. Crandall, one of those qualities is a keen ability to anticipate change. Crandall, the chairman of AMR Corporation, piloted American Airlines through an extremely turbulent era in the air-travel business.

Olympic gymnast Mary Lou Retton got a big boost from her natural enthusiasm. She leapt out of a small town in West Virginia and landed in the hearts of people everywhere.

In the case of Hugh Downs, the veteran ABC newsman, one of these leadership qualities was his down-to-earth humility. Downs managed to build a huge career for himself in the highly competitive business of broadcasting and still remain a gentleman.

Whatever those qualities are for you —a dogged persistence, a steel-trap mind, a great imagination, a positive attitude, a strong sense of values —let them blossom into leadership. And remember that actions are far more powerful than words.

Arthur Ashe was a world-class tennis player and a world-class father—a true leader in those and other realms. He too believed in leading by example.

"My wife and I talk about this with our six-year-old daughter," Ashe said in an interview just before his death. "Children are much more impressed by what they see you do than by what you say," he said. "Children at that age certainly keep you honest. If you have been preaching one thing all along and all of a sudden you don't do it, they're going to bring it right up in your face.

"I tell her it's not polite to eat with your elbows on the table. Then after dinner I'm putting my elbows up. She says, 'Daddy, your elbows are on the table.' You have to be man enough, or woman enough, to say, 'You're right,' and take your elbows down. In fact, that's an even stronger learning experience than her hearing it. It means that she did listen in the past. She understands it. And she recognizes it when she sees it. But it takes actions, rather than mere words, to accomplish that."

A leader establishes standards and then sticks to them. Douglas A. Warner III, for instance, has always insisted on what he calls "full transparency."

"When you come in to make a proposal to me," says Warner, president of J. P. Morgan & Co., Incorporated, "assume that everything that you just told me appears tomorrow on the front page of the Wall Street Journal. Are you going to be proud to have handled this transaction or handled this situation in the way you just recommended, assuming full transparency?

If the answer to that is no, then we're going to stop right here and examine what the problem is." That is a mark of leadership.

Well-focused, self-confident leadership like that is what turns a vision into reality. Just ask Mother Teresa. She was a young Catholic nun, teaching high school in an upper-middle-class section of Calcutta. But she kept looking out the window and seeing the lepers on the street. "I saw fear in their eyes," she said. "The fear they would never be loved, the fear they would never get adequate medical attention."

She could not shake that fear out of her mind. She knew she had to leave the security of the convent, go out into the streets, and set up homes of peace for the lepers of India. Over the years to come, Mother Teresa and her Missionaries of Charity have cared for 149,000 people with leprosy, dispensing medical attention and unconditional love.

One December day, after addressing the United Nations, Mother Teresa went to visit a maximum-security prison in upstate New York. While inside she spoke with four inmates who had AIDS. She knew at once that these were the lepers of today.

She got back to New York City on the Monday before Christmas, and she went straight to City Hall to see Mayor Edward Koch. She asked the mayor if he would telephone the governor, Mario Cuomo. "Governor," she said, after Koch handed her the phone, "I'm just back from Sing Sing, and four prisoners there have AIDS. I'd like to open up an AIDS center. Would you mind releasing those four prisoners to me? I'd like them to be the first four in the AIDS center."

"Well, Mother," Cuomo said, "we have forty-three cases of AIDS in the state prison system. I'll release all forty-three to you."

"Okay," she said. "I'd like to start with just the four. Now let me tell you about the building I have in mind. Would you like to pay for it?"

"Okay," Cuomo agreed, bowled over by this woman's intensity.

Then Mother Teresa turned to Mayor Koch, and she said to him, "Today is Monday. I'd like to open this on Wednesday. We're going to need some permits cleared. Could you please arrange those?"

Koch just looked at this tiny woman standing in his office and shook his head back and forth. "As long as you don't make me wash the floors," the mayor said.

THE FIRST STEP TOWARD SUCCESS IS IDENTIFYING YOUR OWN LEADERSHIP STRENGTHS.

□

Chapter—2
Starting to Communicate

Theodore Roosevelt's children adored him, and they had good reason to. An old friend came to Roosevelt one day in distress. His young son had left home and gone to live with his aunt. The boy was wild. He was this and he was that. And the father claimed that no one could get along with him.

Roosevelt said, "Nonsense. I don't believe there's a thing wrong with the boy. But if a boy with spirit can't get the right sort of treatment at home, he'll go some place else to get it."

Several days later Roosevelt saw the boy and said, "What's all this I hear about your leaving home?"

"Well, Colonel," said the boy, "every time 1 go to Dad he explodes. He's never given me a chance to tell my story. I'm always wrong. I'm always to blame."

"You know, son," said Roosevelt, "you may not believe it now, but your father is your best friend. You are more to him than all the rest of the world."

"That may be, Colonel Roosevelt," the boy said, "but I do wish he'd take some other way of showing it."

Then Roosevelt sent for the father, and he began to tell the father a few shocking truths. The fattier exploded just the way the boy described. "See here," said Roosevelt. "If you talk to your boy the way you've just been talking to me, I don't wonder he left home. I only marvel that he didn't do it before. Now you go and get acquainted with him. Meet him halfway."

—DALE CARNEGIE

Nothing could be easier than failing to communicate. Condescending, contradicting, berating, demeaning, treating other people as if "I am the boss, and you just work here"—until recently these were widely accepted forms of human interaction inside some of the largest and best-known companies in the world. "Barking rights" were thought to be a natural prerogative of executive positions, along with an office window and a two-hour lunch. Families, schools, and other organizations unfortunately followed suit.

For years loudness was equated with toughness. Stubbornness was equated with superior knowledge. Argumentativeness was equated with honesty. We should all—supervisor and employee, parent and child, teacher and student—be grateful those days are finally coming to an end.

Jerry Greenwald, former vice chairman of Chrysler Corporation, compares the old corporate method of communication to a trickle-down version of that childhood game, telephone. "If two teenagers live next to each other and they have something to sort out between them, one crosses the lawn, and they talk it out. If they were two people in two departments of a corporation, the teenager would tell his older brother, who would tell his mother, who would tell his father, who would go next door and tell the father of the other teenager, who would tell the other teenager's mother, and finally the other teenager would get the message and say, 'What was the guy next door trying to tell me?'

"We're trying to break all that down at Chrysler," Greenwald explained while he was still at the auto company. "If you are an operator in a plant and you need to tell someone three hundred feet at the other end of the plant to change something so you can do your job better, go over and tell him. Don't tell your foreman to tell your superintendent to tell his superintendent so that six months from how the other person will still be trying to figure out what you wanted to change."

More and more people, in businesses and elsewhere, are beginning to understand how important good communication really is. The ability to communicate well is what lights the fire in people. It's what turns great ideas into action. It's what makes all achievement possible.

Communicating well is not terribly complicated— not in theory, anyway. Communicating, after all, is something every one of us does every day in our personal lives. We've all been communicating since the early days of childhood. At least we think we have. But true communication, effective communication, is in fact relatively rare in the adult world.

There's no secret recipe for learning to communicate well, but there are some basic concepts that can be mastered with relative ease. Here are the first steps to successful communication. Follow them and you will be on your way.

1. Make communication a top priority.
2. Be open to other people.
3. Create a receptive environment for communication.

No matter how busy you find yourself during the work day, you absolutely must make time to communicate. All the brilliant ideas in the world are worthless if you don't share them. Communication can be accomplished in many ways—in meetings, in face-to-face sessions with colleagues, just walking down the hall, or stopping at the water cooler, or spending half an hour in the company lunchroom. What's most important is that communicating never stop.

Robert Crandall has a big conference room down the hall from his chairman's office at AMR Corporation, the parent company of American Airlines. Every Monday he spends much of his day in there, listening and talking to people from all parts of the company. "Yesterday morning," Crandall said not long ago, "we had the senior officers and eight or ten or twelve other people from three or four levels in the company in there, and we were doing a very complicated analysis.

"We're trying to understand whether or not this hub-and-spoke system that we constructed has become economically indefensible as a consequence of the way the industry is changing. When we created this particular pattern of hubs and spokes, the world looked one way, and now it looks a different way. That's had an effect on how passengers flow across the system. It's also had an effect on pricing. The consequence is that we are not at all sure that the hub-and-spoke system remains viable. Determining that is very complicated.

"It takes an enormous amount of data. So we spent three and a half hours yesterday, in the course of which there were many different points of view expressed and a lot of talking back and forth and a good deal of intense feeling all around. Anyway, we finally sent people away with three or four supplementary assignments, and they'll come back in a couple of weeks with the additional data. Then we'll sit down and talk some more. 'Is what we are doing wrong? And what can we do differently that has the probability of working?' That's how we eventually hope to find our way out of these dilemmas."

The benefits here are twofold: Crandall gets the input of knowledgeable people and they get to help create the future vision of American Airlines. That's fundamental to the development of trusting relationships.

Communication doesn't have to happen in big conference rooms. Some of the best corporate communication occurs in seemingly informal ways. Walter A. Green, the chairman of Harrison Conference Services, Inc., uses a technique he calls his "one-on-ones."

"Unfortunately," Green says, "in organizations we have structures. We have a president, vice presidents, and all these other levels. One-on-ones are a way of overcoming that. These are off-the-record conversations—usually at lunch—where I meet with anyone in the organization I care to meet with. It's a chance for me to stay in touch with what's important to them. How do they feel about the company? How do they feel about their jobs? I'd like to learn something about them as individuals. I like to become more human to them, and I like them to ask me questions about the company. All of that is easier one-on-one." As a result of these conversations, Green's vision for the company begins to grow.

Douglas Warner, the J. P. Morgan president, has brought this practice of direct communication into that old-line bank. "We literally walk around, walk through the inner floor," Warner says. "Go down and see some people. Get out of the office, go to other places instead of insisting that everybody come here."

Several times a week Warner or his top assistant has coffee with thirty or forty of Morgan's top people. "Eyeball-to-eyeball communication, direct and informal," in Warner's words. Even a bank like Morgan has discovered the usefulness of these simple chats. The same theory is applied inside the executive suite. "As part of all that, the managing directors of the firm, three hundred-odd people, would be invited to a large room every day for lunch—the ones who are in New York and the ones who are visiting from overseas. That way there's a real forum every day."

David Luther, corporate director of quality at Corning, Incorporated, describes this process at his organization: "I use the term bottom trawling, going to the bottom of the organization and asking, What's really going on? What are people worried about? What are they saying? What are they up against? What can you do to help?"

The need for effective communication doesn't stop at the office door. It extends to the home, to the school, to the church, even to the halls of science. Any place where people meet with people, communication is key.

It used to be that research scientists could spend their whole lives in the laboratory, single-mindedly searching for the truths of the natural order. But those days are gone. In today's competitive world, even scientists need to listen and talk.

"Many scientists don't know how to effectively communicate what they are doing," says Dr. Ronald M. Evans, an eminent research professor at the Salk Institute for Biological Studies. "They know what they are doing. They have a pretty good idea of why they're doing it. But they have difficulty putting that into perspective, transmitting the ideas outside the laboratory. It's a major limitation at many levels. To obtain funding, you have to convince people that you're doing something that's important."

When Lee Iacocca first went to work at the Ford Motor Company, he discovered the same limitation in many automobile designers and engineers: "I've known a lot of engineers with terrific ideas who had trouble explaining them to other people. It's always a shame when a guy with great talent can't tell the board or a committee what's in his head."

Without mastery of that very basic human skill— the ability to talk and listen to others —members of a company, a school, or a family can't thrive for long.

Things had gotten frenetic around the Levines' house. The children were getting older. That meant play dates, birthday parties, Little League games, gymnastics classes, Brownie troops, religious instruction —and more carpool trips for Harriet than anyone could count.

Stuart had a job he loved, but the travel was grueling and it kept him away from the family more than he would have liked. That left Harriet at home with Jesse and Elizabeth, who were terrific kids but were getting more independent by the day.

"Jesse and Elizabeth were watching far too much television," Harriet recalls, "and they weren't reading nearly enough. We barely had time to communicate."

Before things got really out of hand, the Levines all sat down together one night and came up with a plan. They would form a family council, they decided. Every Sunday after dinner they would gather around the kitchen table and talk in a calm way about whatever was on their minds. "The idea was to have a regular forum for family communication, every week, no matter what," Harriet explains.

The family council began dealing with issues large and small. Are the kids getting in their half hour of reading before television? Is Stuart going to be back in town for the soccer game? When is Harriet going to stop serving that same chicken dish?

At the end of the meeting the children would be given their weekly allowances. "Everyone is supposed to participate, and no one ever gets in trouble - as long as they tell the truth."

The biggest mistake managers used to make— besides thinking that all wisdom flowed from them- was failing to understand that communication absolutely has to be a two-way street. You have to share your ideas with others and listen to theirs. That's step number two: Be open to other people—above, below, and beside.

Publilius Syrus, the Roman playwright, recognized this fact of human nature two thousand years ago. "We are interested in others when they are interested in us," Syrus wrote.

If you can show your colleagues you are receptive to their ideas, they're more likely to be receptive to yours-and to keep you honestly informed about the things you need to know. Show that you care about the future of the organization and that you care as much about them. And don't limit those displays of concern to your coworkers. Communicate the same genuine caring to your customers and your clients too.

At Saunders Karp & Company, merchant banker Thomas A. Saunders III spends his professional life looking for growing companies to invest his clients' funds in. He's an expert at spotting business gems. Nothing impresses Saunders more than a company that really knows how to communicate with its customers.

He recently paid a visit to a wholesale jewelry company in Lafayette, Louisiana. He spent a day touring the company's facilities. But all it really took was five minutes in the telemarketing room for Saunders to recognize a first-string communications success.

"They handled their customers very efficiently on the phone, and the quality of the service was extremely high," Saunders said. "They didn't seem to make any mistakes. It was just bing, bing, bing, 'You want this? .. . Yes, we have that in stock.... You want two of those, fine.... You want three of those, fine. . . . Yes, we have them. . . . No, you have to back-order that.... May I suggest a substitution? .. . Yes, well, if you look on page six hundred of our catalog, there's a mounting. . .' Boom. 'Thank you very much.' It was over in fifteen seconds. Unbelievable."

The average call took fifteen seconds, and the average customer went away thrilled. Who wouldn't put money in a company like that?

It's easy to become isolated from customers and colleagues, especially for those people who rise in an organization. But no matter how high you get, communication still has to run in all directions, talking and listening, up, down, and around the chain of command.

Ronald Reagan wasn't called the Great Communicator for nothing. Throughout his long political career he made it a point to listen and talk to the people he served. Even when he was president, Reagan continued to read constituent mail. He would have his White House secretaries give him a selection of letters each afternoon. At night he would take them up to his quarters and write out personal replies.

Bill Clinton has put the televised town meeting to much the same use: keeping himself informed about how people are feeling and showing people that he cares about them. Even if he doesn't have solutions for all the problems they bring up, there Clinton is, listening, connecting, articulating his own ideas. There's nothing new about any of this. Abraham Lincoln took a similar approach more than a century ago. In those days, any citizen could petition the president. Sometimes Lincoln would ask an aide to respond, but frequently he would answer the petitioners personally.

He took some criticism for that. Why bother when there was a war to be fought, a union to be saved? Because Lincoln knew that understanding public opinion was an essential part of being president, and he wanted to hear it firsthand.

Richard L. Fenstermacher, executive director of North American auto operations marketing at Ford Motor Company, is a firm believer in that. "My door's open," he's constantly telling his people. "If you're walking up the hall and you see me in there, even if you just want to say hi, stop in. If you want to bounce an idea off me, do it. Don't feel you have to go through the managers."

That kind of easy interaction doesn't happen by accident. That's where rule number three comes into play: Create a receptive environment for communication.

It's a basic fact about communicating with people: they won't say what they think—and won't listen receptively to what you say—unless a foundation of genuine trust and shared interest has been laid. You can't be insincere. How you really feel about communication, whether you're open or not, comes through loud and clear, no matter what you say. "You know right away if somebody is approachable or if they're not," Olympic gymnast Mary Lou Retton has said. "When you get that feeling, you can read a person by nonverbal communication and body language. You know when somebody is standing in the corner and saying, 'Hey, I don't want to be talked to.'"

How can you avoid sending that message? Be open, like people, and let them know you do. Follow Retton's advice: "Being down-to-earth and humble is extremely important. I just try to put people at ease. Everybody's the same. I think everybody is on a certain level, whether you are the CEO of a company or a salesperson. It's just a different job." That's what creating a receptive environment is all about: putting people at ease.

It used to be easier than it is today. Television announcer and former baseball great Joe Garagiola remembers how much one-on-one contact there used to be between the players and the fans: "When we used to come off the field and go to our homes after the games, we would ride the subways with the same fans who were in the stands a few hours earlier.

"It wasn't uncommon for one of the fans to say, 'Hey, Joe, why did you swing at that third strike? Why didn't you let it go?' Now there isn't the same personal connection between the fan and the players other than reading about whether or not he's signing a six- or a seven-million-dollar contract."

Ray Stata, the chairman of Analog Devices, Inc., a manufacturer of high-performance integrated circuits, learned the importance of taking a personal interest from his friend Red Auerbach, the long-time president of the Boston Celtics.

Stata recalls, "When he would talk about leadership, he often used the phrase, 'I love my people.' He considered that a real prerequisite to leadership. And they have to know it. So if you have an environment where people genuinely believe that at the end of the day they can trust in your interest and concern about their well-being, then you have created relationships that have more meaning to them." Then, and only then, will the ground be appropriately prepared for communication.

Don't expect this to happen without some work.

Several years ago Coming's David Luther was trying to convince a union leader to embrace the quality-improvement program that the company was trying to start. Luther made his pitch, talking on and on in what he thought was a very convincing way about the importance of quality improvement. This program was going to improve life for both management and labor, Luther promised the union man. But the labor leader clearly wasn't buying a word of what Luther had to say.

Luther recalls, "He got up and he said, 'Give me a break. That's baloney. You guys, that's a scam. It's better than most of your scams, but it's a scam. All you're trying to do is get more out of the workers here.'"

They kept talking, though. "He came around a little," Luther says, "but I didn't convince him, and 1 came to the conclusion that I could never talk my way into his trust. I could only demonstrate that I deserved it. So I said, 'I'm going to be back next year with this, and I'm going to be back the year after that, and I'm going to be back the year after that. I'm going to keep coming back with the same stuff.'" And Luther kept corning back.

His message took several years to sink in, and first he had to show he could be trusted on some smaller issues. He had to show he was listening to their concerns as well. But in the end Luther had the patience to let the message take hold, and Coming's unions became real partners in the quality-improvement program.

One last thing to remember: Once people do take the risk of telling you what they think, don't punish them for their openness. Do nothing —absolutely nothing— to discourage them from taking the risk of communicating again.

"If an employee makes a suggestion that I don't agree with, then I have to be very delicate about the way in which I tell them I don't agree," says Fred J. Sievert, chief financial officer of the New York Life Insurance Company. "I want to encourage them to come back to me the next time and make another suggestion. Now, I told some of the people on my staff that I may disagree with them ninety-nine times out of a hundred, but I want them to keep coming to me with their views. That's what they get paid for. The one time out of a hundred is going to be of value, and I'm not going to view them as any weaker because I disagree with them the other times."

One in a hundred. That may not sound so impressive, but great fortunes have been made on odds less certain than that. That's why listening and sharing ideas is so important.

The truth of the matter is that communication is both a skill and an art. It's a process worth thinking about and practicing more than most people do. It sometimes involves showing personal vulnerability by putting your ideas on the line. You're sharing with others and asking them to share with you. That's not always easy. It takes work and time. Techniques have to be acquired and practiced constantly. But take heart. Practice does make perfect, or very nearly so.

Kuo Chi-Zu is the chief prosecutor in Taipei, Taiwan, and a tremendously compelling public speaker. But he wasn't always so comfortable talking in front of a group. As a rising young prosecutor, Chi-Zu was always being invited to address local organizations. He said no to the Rotary. He said no to the Lions. He said no to Junior Achievement. He was so frightened of the prospect of appearing in public—as many people are—that he turned every invitation down.

"Even if I were just attending a meeting," he remembers, "I always selected the seat at the far corner. And I almost never said a single word."

He knew this fear was slowing the progress of his career—not to mention keeping him awake at night in fits of anxiety. He knew he had to get a grip on his communication problem.

Then one day Chi-Zu was invited to speak at his old high school, and he recognized at once that this was his opportunity. He had, after all, made great effort over the years to maintain a strong relationship with the school and with its students and graduates. If there was any audience he could trust—and that would feel open to what he had to say—this was the one.

So he agreed to appear, and he prepared himself as well as he could. He chose a subject he knew a tremendous amount about and cared deeply for: his job as a prosecutor. He built the speech around real-life examples. He didn't memorize. He didn't write out the words. He just walkedup to the front of the school auditorium and spoke as if he were addressing a room full of friends, which he was.

The speech was a great success. From the podium he could see the eyes in the audience riveted on him. He could hear the people laughing at his jokes. He could feel their warmth and support, and when he was finished speaking, the students rose to their feet for a robust standing ovation.

Chi-Zu learned some valuable lessons about communication that day: how communication takes a certain openness and a trusting environment, what dividends successful communication can pay. Chi-Zu didn't stop there. He became a favorite on the Taipei lecture circuit and was quickly catapulted into the chief prosecutor's job.

He was finally learning to communicate.

COMMUNICATION IS BUILT ON TRUSTING RELATIONSHIPS.

□

Chapter—3
Motivating People

Even as a boy Andrew Carnegie discovered the astonishing importance that people place on their names. When he was ten years old, he had a father rabbit and a mother rabbit. He awoke one morning to discover that he had a whole nest full of little rabbits and nothing to feed them.

What do you suppose he did? Well, he had a brilliant idea. He told half a dozen boys in the neighborhood that if they would go out every day and pull enough dandelions and grass and clover to feed the rabbits, he would name the rabbits in their honor. The plan worked like magic, and here is the point of the story.

Andrew Carnegie never forgot tint incident. And years later, he made millions of dollars by using the same technique in business. He wanted to sell steel rails to the Pennsylvania Railroad. J. Edgar Thomson was president of the railroad then. So Andrew Carnegie, remembering the lesson he had learned from his rabbits, built a huge steel mill in Pittsburgh and called it the J. Edgar Thomson Steel works.

Now let me ask you a question. When the Pennsylvania Railroad needed steel rails after that, where do you suppose J. Edgar Thomson bought them?

—DALE CARNEGIE

Paul Fireman needed a highly motivated work force. Fireman, chairman of Reebok International, made a promise that was unusually bold. In two years' time, Fireman vowed, Reebok would overtake Nike in market share.

Fireman didn't bribe or threaten or cajole the people who worked for him. He led them to motivation. He showed the employees he was willing to take risks, encouraging them to do the same. He built an innovative product-development program and funded it generously. He vowed to spend whatever it took— whatever—to hire the world's top sports figures as Reebok spokespeople. Fireman talked and lived a new Reebok vision, twenty-four hours a day.

"You need to build an enrollment," he explains. "I don't think you can dictate that to people. I don't think you can tell people, 'Go. March. Do this.' What you need to do is to take the time to enroll people in your thinking, your vision, your dream, your fantasy, whatever it is you're doing. Enroll them. It takes time. It takes effort. It takes continual reinforcement. But you don't dictate. You enroll.

"If you enroll one person, then you have a metamorphosis. You change someone, and that person becomes able to enroll ten people. They become able to enroll a hundred people. People thought that my goal was outrageous. But after the second, third, fifth, tenth, twentieth, and thirtieth days, they saw that it's not a statement. It's a way of life.

"It's like the old cowboy movies where the hero was going to make the final battle against the villain and rescue the heroine," explained Fireman. "As the hero was riding on his white horse, with one other guy next to him, a person joined in from the right. Then ten more from the left. And they keep going until finally at the end of the thirty seconds, there are seven hundred people riding, dust flying, and they're on their way to the final shot.

"You can't wait until you call everybody up and say, 'Will you join me at River Creek?' You make them want to come along. You ride. You go. And you just suck everybody else with you. The music rises. And you find that when you get there, whether you needed seven hundred or nine hundred, the point is that you're riding. And they want to ride along." You've got to make them want to ride along. It's a leader's job to foster those feelings. "We are in this together." "We are part of a team." "What we do is valuable." "We're the best." That is the soil that real motivation grows in.

Sure, everyone wants a paycheck, an end-of-the-year bonus, a stock plan, and a great benefits package too. But real motivation will never flow from financial inducements alone, or for that matter, from a fear of being fired. People who work only for a paycheck and not because they like what they do and or feel inspired to do it well—these people will work only as hard as they have to in order to get paid. Fear is just as poor a motivator. Companies that are run on that basis will end up with a work force of resentful employees, just itching to take advantage of the boss.

"There is only one way under heaven to get anybody to do anything," Dale Carnegie said, "and that is by making the other person want to do it. Remember, there is no other way.

"Of course," Carnegie went on, "you can make someone want to give you his watch by sticking a revolver in his ribs. You can make your employees give you cooperation—until your back is turned—by threatening to fire them. You can make a child do what you want by a spanking or a threat. But these crude methods have sharply undesirable repercussions."

So what do people really want? "Not many things," Carnegie said. "Health and the preservation of life. Food. Sleep. Money and the things money will buy. Life in the hereafter. Sexual gratification. The well-being of our children. A feeling of importance.

"Almost all these wants are usually gratified, all except one. There is one longing—almost as deep, as imperious as the desire for food or sleep. It is what Freud calls the desire to be great. It is what Dewey calls the desire to be important."

Give someone a real sense of purpose, the feeling that he or she is working for a valuable, mutually important goal. That's where true motivation comes from—motivation not just to go through the motions of working, motivation to excel.

So recognize people. Include them. Encourage them. Train them. Ask their opinions. Praise them. Let them make decisions. Share the glory with them. Seek their advice and follow it when you can. Make them understand how valued they are. Encourage them to take risks. Give them the freedom to work as they see fit, and convey your belief in their abilities by getting out of the way.

Show people, in other words, that you trust, respect, and care about them. Do that, and you will be surrounded by motivated people.

As Bill Geppert says, "Take care of your people, and the business takes care of itself." Geppert is general manager of Cox Cable, Inc., in New Orleans, a position that makes him responsible for three hundred employees. One of them is a young technical construction specialist named Brian Clemons, who works for Cox in suburban Jefferson Parish.

Clemons was on vacation one morning, and he happened to stop in at a Home Depot store to buy some lumber. While waiting for his lumber to be cut, he overheard a man complaining about Cox. As the man spoke, eight or nine other Home Depot customers were gathered around, listening to this tale of cable-television woe.

"Now, Brian could have done a number of things," Geppert said later, recounting what happened next. "He was on vacation. He had work to do, and his wife wanted him home. So he could have just gone about his business, ignoring what was being said. What did Brian do? Brian Clemons walked right up and said, 'Sir, I couldn't help but overhear what you were telling these folks. I work for Cox. Would you please give me an opportunity to make the situation right? In fact, I guarantee we can take care of your problem.'

"Well, you can imagine the looks on those eight people's faces. They were astonished. Brian, who wasn't wearing his uniform, walked over to a pay phone, called the office, and dispatched a repair crew to the house. The repair crew met that customer as he arrived home and took care of the situation to the customer's satisfaction. In fact, we found out later that Brian even went a step further. He followed up when he came back to work to make sure that the customer was satisfied with the result. And he gave the customer two weeks' credit on his account and an apology for the inconvenience."

A rare event? In some organizations, service like that is unheard-of. For employees to take that kind of responsibility? To get involved in issues that aren't technically their jobs? To "waste" their own vacation time? Unlikely. But Geppert has been working to make that attitude standard at Cox. He has helped his employees understand that Cox is their company, and its success will bring their success. "Now, this may be a blazing flash of common sense," Geppert says, "but that's the kind of thing we want people to get involved in and do."

So how can you force employees to take that kind of interest in their jobs? The answer is, you can't. People can never be forced to do an extraordinary job. They will perform extraordinarily only if they want to. The challenge is giving them a reason to want to.

"Action springs out of what we fundamentally desire," Harry A. Overstreet wrote in his timeless book, Influencing

Human Behavior. "The best piece of advice which can be given to would-be persuaders, whether in business, in the home, in the school, in politics is: 'First, arouse in the other person an eager want. He who can do this has the whole world with him. He who cannot walks a lonely way.'" Over-street's insight remains true today.

David McDonald, president of Pelco Corporation, a successful security-equipment company on the West Coast, has done a splendid job of instilling this want-to attitude. He treats his people with dignity. He communicates corporate values they can believe in. He gives his employees the autonomy to decide how to get the job done. The results have been extraordinary.

"We have an employee named Bill Reese who works in the sales department," McDonald says. "Bill got a call one Friday morning from a customer in Seattle. This fellow was frantic. He thought he had ordered a special run of security equipment from us months earlier for a real important installation, I believe for a boating company.

"As he was coming down to the tail end of his installation, he realized he didn't have the Pelco equipment. He realized he had never ordered it in the first place. The job was supposed to be completed the next day, Saturday, or he was going to be into a very heavy financial penalty. He didn't know what to do. We were the only source of this equipment. He called and talked to Bill fairly early in the morning. This is one of the few products that we actually custom manufacture for each order. There were none in stock, and they required a specific hammer to be installed in-house. Bill took the call and said he'd do the best he could.

"Bill went into our factory and bypassed the whole production-control system; he started a production job from scratch and got everybody tuned in. I think the quantity of this order was fifteen. He got the project into high gear through our fabrication department. But then we weren't going to have the cameras by the time it got to assembly. So he contacted our supplier in Los Angeles and arranged to have fifteen of these cameras shipped counter to counter from Los Angeles. He had somebody literally take them to LAX as soon as he hung up the phone. They arrived a few hours later in Fresno, and he was at the airport to pick them up. Bill picked up the cameras and got them to assembly just in time to get them installed into these housings that actually came off the assembly line about fifteen minutes before we had to have them at the airport.

"Bill had made arrangements with United Airlines to make room on their plane up to San Francisco for this product so it could be shipped counter to counter to our customer up in Seattle. Well, as it worked out, Bill and a group of other people took these housings to the airport. But there had been a shift change, and the United person whom Bill had spoken to no longer was there. The new person didn't have any idea what was going on. He and Bill had a big argument. Meanwhile the guy looked over his shoulder and said, 'Well, it doesn't matter anyhow because it's too late. There goes the plane right now, backing away from the gate.'

"Having come as far as he had with this, Bill was not going to be denied. He ran through the United Airlines freight depot onto the ramp. By this time the plane was moving under its own power, taxiing toward the runway. Bill caught up with the airplane. Got in front of it. Got the pilot's attention. This was a 737 jet. Got the plane to stop. The pilot almost—well, you know what he almost did. They took the plane back to the gate. And after all that effort, Bill actually managed to get the product on the plane. Our customer got his product later that evening in Seattle and completed his installation the next day."

What makes this incident even more impressive, McDonald recalls, was that "during this whole time, none of it was under management's direction. Management was not even aware that any of this had happened until it was all over. You can't make people do that. You have to make them want to do that."

And people will only want to perform like that if they feel like an important part of the organization. That's why employees need to be respected and included in a corporate vision they can embrace. That's why people need a stake in their work lives. That's why their successes need to be rewarded, praised, and celebrated. That's why their failures need to be handled gingerly. Do those things. Then stand back and watch the results roll in.

There's nothing new about this concept. Dwight Eisenhower was asked once about his secret for taming the fractious Congress. Did the former general mention military discipline or the might-makes-right power of the presidency? Not even close. He talked about persuasion. "You do not lead by hitting people over the head," he said. "That's assault, not leadership."

Eisenhower added, "I would rather persuade a man to go along because once he has been persuaded, he will stick. If I scare him, he will stay just as long as he is scared, and then he is gone."

This power of persuasion was never more important than it is today. Apple Computer understood that. So did Corning. So do most of the other well-led companies out there. Get people interested in what they're doing. Truly make it theirs. They'll work and work, and then they'll work some more.

Once this basic principle is recognized and understood, it's really quite easy to dream up all kinds of specific motivation techniques. But three important concepts of human behavior underlie them all.

1. Employees must be included in all parts of the process, every step of the way. Teamwork is the key here, not hierarchy.

2. People must be treated as individuals. Always acknowledge their importance and show them respect. They're people first, employees second.
3. Superior work must be encouraged, recognized, and rewarded. Everyone responds to expectations. If you treat people as if they are capable and smart—and get out of the way—that's exactly how they'll perform.

Include people. At the traditional kind of big corporation, people often felt a little disconnected. Each was just a number, one of thousands, a human cog in a giant industrial wheel. There are literally hundreds of stories out there, told so often they've become legend, about disgruntled employees calling in sick or spending more time on break than at their desks. If a company's employees feel that way, that company is poorly led. Its goals have not become their goals. No company can succeed in a situation like that.

Successful leaders today involve employees in all aspects of the work process: design, manufacture, inventory, marketing. Leaders create teams. They don't issue orders from above. Leaders realize that the employees who actually do the work can actually make decisions. Certainly, employees who are engaged in real decision making respond better than those who are not.

American Airlines, widely regarded as the best-run company in that tumultuous industry, has institutionalized a kind of consensus management. Chairman Robert Crandall explains: "This whole notion of companies this size being run entirely at the will of a single entity is nonsensical. Maybe there are compares that are run that way, but I don't think so. For the most part, companies like this one are run on the basis of a consensus judgment. In the end, the chief executive always has to make the decision and bear the responsibility for it. But my job is much more a matter of exploring options and bringing a group together and seeking consensus among the members of that group than it is dictating solutions."

Martin Edelston, president of Boardroom Reports, runs his business newsletter publishing company in the same consensus way—by constantly seeking suggestions from his sixty-five employees.

"You notice when you walk around," Edelston says, "none of us here is a rocket scientist. These are all very ordinary people." So how did these "ordinary people" produce such extraordinary results? "1 asked everybody for two ideas to make our meetings more interesting," Edelston explains. "Now, we've had thousands of ideas from these people on every subject imaginable."

The whole work force is driven by suggestions, a modification of the Japanese kaizen system for continuous improvement. "If I asked you for two ways in which I can be better, you'd be complimented," Edelston said. "You would tell me how I could make this better. You'd feel really good if I implemented it. I go back next week, ask for two more, and then two more, so that something is happening. I've taken sixty-five people and made giants out of them. So we have a company now that's doing over a million dollars' worth of business per person."

Steven Jobs and Steven Wozniak followed a similarly nonhierarchical approach when they began putting together Apple Computer's executive team. They weren't so concerned about who was the boss. Peter O. Crisp, managing partner of Venrock Associates, a venture capital firm that got behind Apple in the early days, still smiles at the founders' unorthodox style: "They would say to themselves, 'We have this device, which has some electronic parts that hopefully we're going to make many copies of. We need to manufacture them at low cost, and they need to be very reliable. What company in the country is the best manufacturer of technical products that have those characteristics?'"

Hewlett-Packard, they concluded. "Jobs and Wozniak would say, 'Well, let's go find the vice president of manufacturing for Hewlett-Packard, and let's hire him.'

"They would try to find the vice president of Hewlett-Packard," Crisp said. "If they couldn't get him, they'd try to find out who his assistant was, or they would find out which of Hewlett-Packard's plants was the best run. They would go and find out who the manufacturing person was there. They'd go and try to hire him. They gave these people generous options awards. So they would attract an experienced person, and then they'd say, 'Okay, now tell us what to do.' Then the Apple people would assist the newcomer in implementing his plans."

Crisp recalls, "They hired a marketing person that way and a manufacturing person, a human-resources person. They were off to the races. You know, on occasion in a startup, the founder is the chief scientist. He may be reluctant to hire a chief operating officer because he may not want to give away too much stock or too much of his authority and have anybody there who can really challenge him. Entrepreneurs can be very possessive of what they have. In this case it was exactly the opposite. It was, 'Let's go.'" And go they did, by engaging their people in the company.

To achieve Apple like results, you've got to follow rule number two. Become interested in your employees and let them know that you are. Treat people like people. That's the second basic concept of motivation.

"Be nice to your people and treat them with respect," says Pelco's David McDonald. "Invest liberally in your people, and don't expect this automatically to produce new profits. Rather take full advantage of your newly enhanced human resources by establishing new extreme-type expectations for your people that translate into exceptional performance for customers and therefore generate more profits."

Say hello. Smile. Get to know your employees. "Employees should be handled like family," says Joyce Harvey, president of Harmon Associates Corporation, a wholly owned subsidiary of Fort Howard Corporation. "You can't expect people to do things that you wouldn't do yourself. You've got to care about them sincerely. Then you can get the same level of respect back."

Harvey goes on, "My former boss used to have a chart in his office. He'd flip it, and it had every employee who worked here. He knew them by name, and he knew their families; he knew what was happening. He'd walk through the mill and say, 'Hi, Joe,' 'Hi, Sam,' 'Hi, Mary.' He let them know that he cared." That may sound old-fashioned, but it's even more important today.

The third basic concept of motivation is just as important as the other two: Acknowledge a job well done. Don't be the tight-lipped, disapproving parent many of us grew up with. Those were the parents who didn't congratulate their kids for getting that A on the report card. They just expected it. Remember how disappointing that was? Well, it's still disappointing. There's still a little child in every one of us, waiting to be praised. So don't forget: People want to be told when they've done a good job. Use praise liberally and often.

There are literally dozens of simple techniques for celebrating successes. At Cox Cable, Bill Geppert seems to use just about every last one. "We have rallies," Geppert says. "We have meetings. We do skits during our monthly meeting to reinforce that message and keep those visible targets and goals in front of our folks. We have celebrations. We load people up in army trucks and drive them across town and talk about how we're going to be competitive with the tougher competitors. We've had fireworks in our celebrations, performers brought in to exemplify the excellence we strive for. We have speakers, awards. We give away money at employee meetings. Any way to get people involved and excited."

John P. Imlay, Jr., chairman of Dun & Bradstreet Software Services, Inc., has his own method for rewarding employees. "I had a theme all through my career," he recalls. "It was very simple: People are the key. I had Tiffany & Co. create a little key which we all wore in our lapels. Sounds a little corny. But at the time, we'd come through bankruptcy, and I wanted to reward those people. The people took it with great emotion. A silver key, if you were with us less than five years. You got a gold when you hit five years. The women got a diamond for ten years."

However you do it, do it. Let the people in your life know that you respect them, that you appreciate their work, that they are important to you and that you want them to learn, grow, and reach their potential.

Motivation, that's called.

MOTIVATION CANNEVERBE FORCED. PEOPLE HAVE TO WANT TO DO A GOOD JOB.

□

Chapter —4

Expressing Genuine Interest in Others

Why read this book? Why not study the technique of the greatest winner of friends the world has ever known? Who is he? You may meet him tomorrow coming down the street. When you get within ten feet of him, he will begin to wag his tail. If you stop and pat him, he will almost jump out of his skin to show you how much he likes you. And you know that behind this show of affection on his part, there are no ulterior motives. He doesn't want to sell you any real estate, and he doesn't want to marry you.

Did you ever stop to think that a dog is the only animal that doesn't have to work for a living? A hen has to lay eggs. A cow has to give milk, and a canary has to sing. But a dog makes his living by giving out nothing but love.

You can make more friends in two months by becoming genuinely interested in other people than you can in two years by trying to get others interested in you. Let me repeat that. You can make more friends in two months by becoming interested in other people than you can in two years by trying to get other people interested in you.

Yet I know and you know people who blunder through

life trying to badger other people into becoming interested in them. Of course, it doesn't work. People are not interested in you. They are not interested in me. They are interested in themselves— morning, noon, and after dinner.

—DALE CARNEGIE

Lynn Povich, editor-in-chief of Working Woman magazine, spent twenty-five years of her life at Newsweek. She started as a secretary, moved up to researcher, and eventually became the first woman ever named a Newsweek senior editor. This put her in the position of supervising writers and editors she had once worked for as a researcher. "It was an interesting turn of events," Povich says.

Most of her colleagues reacted quite well to the promotion, all except one of the six section editors who now reported to her. Povich recalls, "He was against the idea from the very beginning—not because he disliked me, but because he felt that I had gotten the job only because I am a woman and that I probably didn't have the credentials for it. He didn't say anything to me, but I heard from several other people that that's what he thought."

Povich tried not to let this bother her. She immersed herself in the new job. She helped develop story ideas. She spent time talking to the writers. She expressed a sincere interest in each of the sections she was responsible for—medicine, media, television, religion, lifestyle, and ideas.

Then one day, about six months after Povich's appointment, her big critic walked into her office and sat in a chair across from her desk. "I have to tell you something," he said to her. "I was totally against this move. I thought you were too young. I thought you didn't have the experience. I thought you got the promotion only because you were a woman.

"But I want to say I really appreciate the interest you've shown in the work, in the writers, and in the section editors.

I've had four guys who were senior editors before you. It was clear to me they were all using this as a stepping-stofle for the next position. None of them genuinely cared, It's absolutely clear that you really are interested, and you show that interest to everyone. "Not surprisingly, Povich has brought that same management style—developed over the years—into her new job at Working Woman. "You have to take people seriously," she explains. "First of all, you can't be remote. You have to touch base with them on a regular basis. I do a lot of walking around and talking to people. We have a system of regular meetings so that everyone here knows there's a particular time, a particular week, when they're actually going to be alone with me. They'll have their time to say whatever they want to. I'm available. I'm interested in what they're doing, I'm interested in their work, and I'm interested in them as people."

Expressing genuine interest in others—there's no better way to make people interested in you. People respond to people who are sincerely interested in them. They can't help but respond.

This is one of the most basic facts of human psychology. We are flattered by other people's attention. It makes us feel special. It makes us feel important. We want to be around people who show interest in us. We want to keep them close. We tend to reciprocate their interest by showing interest in them.

Monsignor Tom Hartman has become something of a legend among young Roman Catholics on Long Island, New York. He has, over the years, been asked to perform more than thirty-eight hundred weddings and to baptize more than ten thousand newborn babies. Why do all these people keep turning to the Monsignor? Aren't there any other priests out there to choose from? Of course there are, but few manage to show the intense interest in other people that Hartman is so well know for.

Hartman doesn't preside over assembly-line wedding ceremonies. He takes a more studied, individual, personal approach. He wants to know everything he possibly can about the two people who have come to him to be married. He invites them to the rectory. He visits their homes. Over a period of several months, he leads them through a series of conversations about themselves. That way, he can tailor a wedding that will fit their personal interests and needs.

"Yes, I'll do your wedding," he tells these couples, "but I don't want it to be just a ritual. I want to discover the mystery here. I want this to be the best wedding possible for you. I want to know about you. I want to talk with you about what you've discovered about your relationship, what you love about each other. I want to learn about the struggles you've had and how you got through those struggles. And I'm going to communicate that at your wedding."

A Hartman wedding isn't the quickest and easiest trip to the altar. But Hartman's personal interest pays major dividends for these couples. Through his caring, they learn new things about each other. "When people see that I am so interested in an important moment in their lives, they began to listen to me on other levels too," he said.

Hartman takes the same personal approach when asked to perform a baptism. He wants to know about the family, about the child, about all the things that make this birth so special to those involved. He has gone so far as to attend Lamaze classes with one single mother whose baby he was going to baptize.

That one expression of interest, he says, has given him an added degree of credibility when he encourages prospective fathers to go through this preparation as well. By attending classes himself, Hartman says, "I was able to get on the trust level with so many men and say, 'Do it. It will introduce you to mystery.' Many men have come back to me later, thrilled they'd done it, and said, 'If I never had that experience, I would be on the outside looking in.'"

There are many different ways of showing interest, and most of them are much easier than attending Lamaze classes. An expression of interest can be as simple as using a pleasant voice on the telephone. When someone calls, say hello in a tone that implies, "I'm happy to hear from you." When you see a familiar face at the shopping mall, greet the person and express a genuine pleasure at the coincidence.

Smile at people. Learn their names and how to pronounce them. Get the spellings and the titles right. Remember their birthdays. Ask about their husbands and wives and children. "I always knew that Clarence Michalis was at Bristol-Myers," says David S. Taylor, secretary-treasurer of H. G. Wellington & Company, Inc., an investment-brokerage firm. "The minute we met, that would click. I remember those two things together. Not everybody does. I have a memory bank that would connect people with businesses."

You never know when these names will come in handy. Taylor learned this lesson when he was working as an executive in the beverage industry. "When I worked for Canada Dry," he said, "it may be hard to think why, but it was important for\ me to know people in the airline industry. They were a big customer. Grumman Aircraft fed a lot of people, and they had a lot of vending machines that dispensed drinks.

"It was just an entree. You could call up and say, 'Look, I'm having a problem with such-and-such.' Remembering these names and having those connections was enormously helpful."

Taylor used this technique as the basis for forming genuine relationships with people. By taking the time to remember people's names and associations, he has been able to help bring people together and solve their problems.

Don't limit those expressions of interest to the so-called important people in your life. Chances are they already get plenty of attention. Don't forget the secretaries, the assistants, the receptionists, the messengers, and all the other under recognized people who keep your life on track. Ask about their days. It's the right thing to do—and you'll be surprised how much quicker the mail arrives at your desk in the morning.

Interest in people has always been a personal trademark of Adriana Bitter, president of Scalamandre Silks. One day Bitter was walking through the wallpaper-print area. She overheard the head of Scalamandre's wallpaper department talking to an employee. "How are you, Louie?" the department head asked.

"Oh, not too well," Louie answered. "I've been suffering from a depression."

"Do you know why?" Bitter asked him, walking up.

"I have this fear of heights and fear of being closed in," Louie explained. "I have to get on a plane and fly to Puerto Rico for my Christmas vacation, and I'm frightened."

Bitter asked a few more questions. "I think it's a good idea if you see a doctor about this," she said finally.

"I went to see a doctor, and I had to go up to the thirty-second floor, and I was so afraid."

"Maybe you'd better find a doctor on the first floor," Bitter told him.

"You know, I had a dream the other night, Mrs-Bitter," he said. "I dreamed that I was so frightened, and you came up and put your arms around me and told me not to worry."

So Bitter put her arms around him and said, "Don't worry, Louie. It will go away. Take some deep breaths."

They talked some more. He started to laugh, and he said, "Will you come on the plane with me?"

Bitter laughed with him.

"He left yesterday," she said a few days later. "So I guess he's doing fine."

People will respond immediately to a genuine expression of warmth. So be sincere. Honest, heartfelt interest has to be built up over time.

A great way to open a conversation—even a business conversation—is to notice an item that relates somehow to the person you're speaking with. It could be a drawing on the office wall, a, desktop pencil holder made by a child, a squash racquet leaning in the corner of the room. Make a comment that shows interest, admiration, or warmth. Or ask a question of a similar kind. "That's a beautiful picture. Who's the artist?" Or "What a thoughtful gift. Is that from one of your children?" Or "Squash? Isn't that a hard game to learn?" There's nothing profound about any of those remarks. But every one of them shows a basic, personal interest in the other person, and it connects in a positive, tasteful way.

Such displays of interest are the fundamental building blocks of successful human relationships. They are the little details that say, "You are important to me. I'm interested. I care." Very few people in this world mind hearing that.

Everything was going well for Steven and Robin Weiser. Steven ran a successful insurance agency. They had a lovely suburban home. He was a consistently generous philanthropist. The couple's oldest daughter was in her first year at Yale, and the younger twins were doing great in high school.

Then one Saturday night as Steven and Robin were eating at a restaurant, he had a massive heart attack and died. He was just forty-five years old.

The funeral was packed with hundreds of people Steve Weiser had touched—his friends, his business associates, officials from the many charities he supported. Many of these people made condolence calls at the Weiser home.

What was nearly as shocking as Steven's untimely death was something his wife said that night. "It's a shame that Steven didn't know how many people he touched, how many people loved him," Robin Weiser said.

Steven Weiser? With all those friends and associates? After all that charity work? Apparently few of these people had ever told him how they felt.

Don't make the same mistake. When you care about someone —a friend, a spouse, a colleague—by all means let that person know. And do it while you have the chance.

Even more important than expressing interest is showing it. Harrison Conference Services, Inc., is in the business of organizing meetings and seminars, worrying about all the logistics so the clients can keep their minds focused on thereal work at hand. To thrive, a company like Harrison must show its guests, over and over again, that the staff is genuinely— almost single-mindedly—interested in them.

It's not enough to have beautiful conference facilities, as Harrison certainly does. It's not enough to have attractive rooms, first-rate cuisine, high-tech audiovisual equipment, or a plethora of recreational choices, all of which Harrison has. Unless the guests feel they're being treated with genuine interest and respect, they'll take their business elsewhere.

"I remember a guest who was attending one of our international programs, a man from China," says Walter A. Green, Harrison's chairman. "One of our people, a hostess, overheard him saying he missed the food of his native country. Well, the hostess happened to be a Chinese chef on the side. The next day she went home and prepared some special Chinese food," and brought the dishes into work. "I can't tell you how taken he seemed by this personal concern for his comfort and by the thrill of being able to share his own cuisine with the people at his table."

What the hostess's action said was, "We are interested—genuinely interested, consistently interested—in you." Who wouldn't appreciate that kind of attention?

Thankfully, this way of relating is a habit easily learned and very gratifying. All it takes is the realization of how important it is and a little bit of practice. Try it with the next person you meet: "Whatever happened to that summer house you were thinking of buying?" Or "What a great view you have in here. How do you stop yourself from staring out the window all day?"

Once you start this process, it will quickly become a natural part of your life. Before you know it, you'll be expressing interest, showing interest, and really becoming more interested in the people around you. The added benefit is that a genuine interest in others will take you outside yourself and make you less focused on whatever your own problems are. The more you stay focused on other people, the more rewarding your personal relationships will be and the fewer negative thoughts you will have. Not a bad payback for a few kind words.

Best-selling business author Harvey B. Mackay started out his career in the envelope industry. That's where he learned many of the lessons that make up his best-selling books. "I'm very strong on creative gifts," Mackay says, "and when I say a gift, I'm not talking about something that's expensive and costs money."

Mackay had an envelope salesman, "a man who in my judgment was just a C-plus salesman," he recalls. "I remember him telling me that one of his buyers had a baby girl, so he went down and bought a gift. Fine, that's wonderful. But the gift was not for the baby girl. It was for the jealous brother at home. He was a year and half, just a piddly little thing. But I remember, that one creative gesture stuck with me right away. All of a sudden I didn't think of him as a C-plus anymore. Now he's our key sales manager."

Expressing this kind of interest in others is especially important when you're the new kid on the block. It was as if Bill Clinton already knew that when he showed up for his first day of kindergarten. He was, his teacher has said, naturally friendly and disarming-ly interested in the other children.

"Hi," he went around saying. "I'm Bill. What's your name?" Corny? Maybe. But then none of his classmates in Hope, Arkansas, expressed any surprise when little Billy was elected president of the United States.

An open, friendly, interested greeting is just as important when you're the new person in the office or the new business-owner in town. The message should not be, I'm here, now what can you do for me? It should be instead, I'm here, now what can I do for you?

So volunteer at the local hospital. Sign up as a Little League coach. Join the PTA. Get involved in a local charity. These are all ways of showing interest in the community, of saying, "I care about this place." Any one of these will help you meet new people in a comfortable environment. It will be fun. It will make you feel good about yourself. It will help you develop new relationships, gain self-confidence, and it will bring you out of your comfort zone.

Dale Carnegie understood this. "If you want others to like you," he wrote, "if you want to develop real friendships, if you want to help others at the same time as you help yourself, keep this principle in mind: Become genuinely interested in other people."

On this score there is no doubt that Carnegie practiced what he preached, even at home with his family. J. Oliver Crom, who is now president of Dale Carnegie & Associates, Inc., discovered this the first time he met his future in-laws.

"To say I was nervous about meeting Dale Carnegie would be an understatement," Crom remembers. "Well, within seconds of meeting him, he had me relaxed, talking about myself, and the way he did that was by asking me questions." Carnegie merely expressed interest in the, gentleman young Rosemary had brought home.

"First of all I said, 'Well, Mr. Carnegie, it's very nice to meet you.' And he said, 'Oh, please, call me Dale. Mr. Carnegie sounds so formal.' And then he said, 'I understand you were born in Alliance, Nebraska.' I said, 'Yes, that's right' And he said, "Tell me, do the same wonderful people live in Alliance that lived there so many years ago when I sold in that territory?' And I said, 'Yes, they do.' He said, 'Well, tell me about some of the people out there, and tell me about yourself.' So he got me talking about myself and about Alliance."

Things progressed swiftly from there. "We took walks in the parks together. We went down and worked in his rose garden. We went to the theater together. He and I rode the subway into the city. We went to see The Seven Year Itch, which was on Broadway at the time. I don't remember much about the play, but I remember, when we went for a walk in Forest Hills Gardens, he knew everyone in the little park. He knew the policeman. He knew all the people walking their dogs and called them by name. They all stopped and greeted him. I didn't know at the time thatthis was so unusual. Coming from the Midwest, I thought that's the way people are."

Stephen Ghysels, who is now a vice president at the Bank of America, learned the hard way how important it is to take a genuine interest in others.

Ghysels got an impressively early start on the fast track. Back in the late 1980s, fresh out of college, he was already an officer at a large investment firm. He had an Art Deco condo on the west side of Los Angeles and a Mercedes in the driveway—all by age 25. "I thought I had it all and I let people know. I had a real attitude.

"But just as the recession was approaching in 1990," Ghysels says, "my boss called me into the office and said, 'Steve, it's not your performance. It's your attitude. People in this office just don't like working with you. I'm afraid we are going to have to part company.'

"It hit me like a rock. I, Mr. Success, was being fired. I knew it wouldn't take me very long to find another high-paying executive position. Wrong. Welcome to the recession, Steve!

"After several frustrating months of job searching, the attitude layer peeled off and revealed a thick layer of fear. For the first time in my life I lacked confidence and was gripped by an intense fear. Since I had previously alienated everyone, I had nowhere to turn, no one to talk to. I was alone."

Only then did Ghysels learn to be interested in others. He started listening. He started caring about something other than himself. He gained a perspective on his own trouble, meeting people who were far worse off than himself. He opened himself up and became more human, more likable, and infinitely more employable.

"I began to look at other people in a different light," he recalls. "My attitude changed. I felt differently. My fear was reduced. My mind was opened. And people began to take notice. The quality of my life was better, even though I had to sell the condo and the Mercedes. "Three years later, I once again have an officer-level job—only this time I'm surrounded by coworkers I can honestly call my friends."

THERE'S NOTHING MORE EFFECTIVE AND REWARDING THAN SHOWING A GENUINE INTEREST IN OTHER PEOPLE.

□

Chapter—5

Seeing Things From the other Person's Point of View

I wanted a private secretary last year, and I put an ad in the paper under a box number. I bet I got three hundred replies. Almost all of them began something like this: "This is in reply to your ad in Sunday's Times under Box 299. I wish to apply far the position you offer. I am twenty-six years old, etc. ..."

But one woman was smart. She didn't talk about what she wanted. She talked about what I wanted. Her letter read like this: "Dear Sir: You will probably get two or three hundred letters in reply to your ad. You are a busy man. You haven't time to read all of them. So if you will just reach for your telephone right now and call Vanderbilt 3-9512," or whatever it was, "I'll be glad to come over and open the letters and throw the worthless ones in the wastebasket and place the others on your desk for your attention. I have had fifteen years experience..."

She then went on to tell about the important men she had worked for. The moment I got that letter, I felt like dancing on the table. 1 immediately picked up the telephone and told her to come over, but I was too late. Some other employer had grabbed her. A woman like that has the business world at her feet.

— DALECARNEGIE

Long before ad man Burt Manning ever set foot on Madison Avenue, he wanted to be a writer. Not a copywriter, an author. So young Manning slaved over a typewriter every day, producing short stories and novels and what he was sure were gut-wrenching plays. But like most young writers, Manning couldn't come close to supporting himself with his words. He needed a job to pay the bills.

Door-to-door selling was the best idea he could find.

He sold Encyclopedia Britannica's. He sold high-end kitchenware. He even went door-to-door in the old working-class neighborhoods of his native Chicago, selling cemetery property.

That last product turned out to be the most profitable of all—but not at first. It wasn't for lack of trying. Every evening after a full day at the typewriter, Manning put on a suit and tie. He packed his salesman's case. And he pressed his most enthusiastic cemetery pitch on the people who answered his knocks: how cemetery property offered strong investment advantages, how Chicago's rapid population growth would surely produce a scarcity of cemetery property, how his company's five-year buy-back guarantee made this a no-risk deal.

"It was actually a very good, low-cost investment, and I believed in it. But I couldn't sell a thing. I wasn't coming at it from their point of view. Instead of focusing on their most important concerns, I kept focusing on the financial aspects. But with the product I was selling, there was something much more relevant that I hadn't thought about."

Manning had failed to ask himself the most basic questions. "I had to say, 'What's really of concern to these folks? What separates them in their views from other people I might know? What do I have to offer that will make them feel good about themselves and feel good about what they are doing for their families?'" The process, as far as Hayes is concerned, begins before a potential customer even steps inside a Lerner store. "In some malls we have seventy-foot lease fronts," she said. "The customer, within eight-point-five seconds, is going to decide whether to walk into that store or just go past it." That instant decision, multiplied millions of times, will determine in large measure whether Lerner is a success. Or as Hayes looks at it, "I've got eight-point-five seconds."

The highly competitive retailing industry has really been the leader in seeing the world from the customer's point of view.

We've all been inside a poorly run store. All the clerks are huddled together, talking to each other. An approaching customer feels like an intruder in some private club. Service? You want service? The sales clerks are far too bored, far too annoyed, or far too busy to be interrupted for something like that.

The era of apathetic customer service has finally begun to pass. Customers said enough. Stores that don't adapt to the new customer-is-everything ethic tend now to go out of business fast, taking their aloof employees with them.

The late Sam Walton hired full-time "greeters" for his Wal-Mart discount stores, people whose sole job was to stand near the front door, say hello to customers, and point them in the right direction. Why? It wasn't just Walton's Arkansas hospitality. He had enough sense to see his own business as the customers do. Here they are, stepping into this huge, brightly lit store, with aisle after aisle of merchandise and no idea which way to go. People need guidance. They appreciate the store that provides it. And if they can locate the merchandise that they're looking for, they are more likely to buy it. That'll delight the customers, which will be good for the store. A delighted customer is good for any store.

"Exceed your customers' expectations." That was always one of Sam Walton's rules. "If you do, they'll come back over and over. Give them what they want and a little more." At retailing's upper end, the Nordstrom chain managed to sail through the recession of the late 1980s and the early 1990s. The department store's number-one priority: see things the customer's way.

"Nordstrom is the most feared retailer in the world," says business consultant Denis E. Waitley. "My wife, Susan, has discovered them as her greatest ally. She bought two pairs of Nordstrom shoes and took them back after she wore them for two weeks. One of the pair hurt, and they took them both back. No problem. Can do. The customer is always king and queen. Customers are royalty, treated the way we want to be treated. That's the way it works."

Even so, Waitley wasn't prepared for the early evening phone call he got at home one night. A friendly-sounding woman was on the line.

She: "Hello, may I speak to Susan Waitley, please? This is Martha, your Nordstrom customer-service representative."

He: "Martha, you're a commissioned sales rep trying to make extra points. What do you want? I'm getting ready to eat, and I don't allow interruptions during dinner. What is it you want Susan for?"

She: "The shoes came in at the store in Susan's size and color, and I'm delivering them after work."

He: "As I remember, you live in South County. We're in North County, which is out of your way. I'll be eating in five minutes, which won't allow you enough time to come by. But thank you for trying."

She: "I'm calling from my cellular phone in your driveway."

He: "Oh, come or in:"

So Nordstrom made a sale, and even Waitley had to admit he was impressed. The store was looking at things in terms of the customer's interests.

It isn't How can we do business in a manner most convenient to us? It is How can we do business in the way most convenient to you? Delighting the customer—that's what it's all about. And there's no way to make all those judgments without looking through the potential customer's eyes.

For every product it sells, Dun & Bradstreet Software Services, Inc., creates a "customer council."

"We do not build a product until the customer council has instructed us that this is their priority," explains John Imlay, the company's chairman. "They come with a priority list. We come with one, the features and functions. We want to be competitive and they want to satisfy their needs. They give us input and we take pride in solving their problems and satisfying their needs."

This is not considered a luxury at Dun & Brad-street. It's a basic part of doing business. "We could not develop a product without customer input," Imlay declares. "There would be an ivory tower, and then we'd be no good."

This outward-looking perspective shouldn't be reserved only for customers. It applies as well to employees, to suppliers, to anyone else you come into contact with every day.

David Holman runs the export division of John Holman & Co. Pty. Ltd., an Australian produce vendor. One day Holman had the unhappy task of calling up one of his biggest growers with a piece of terrible news: the new export price for the man's vegetables was going to be half what was originally expected.

This generated the predictable reaction on the phone. The man sounded aghast. The situation seemed serious enough that Holman decided to drive the two hours to the man's farm and finish the discussion in person.

When he got to the farm, the fields were wet and muddy, and the grower was out with the crop. So Holman borrowed a spare pair of the grower's rubber boots and marched out to meet him in the field.

"How are you doing?" Holman asked the grower in a concerned tone of voice. Then he listened with true empathy about all the hard work the grower had put in, about the time that had gone into this year's crop, about the economic hardship of being on the land in the 1990s, about his disappointment over the current price.

Holman had no trouble understanding the grower's point of view. The grower clearly had major problems on his hands. Holman just expressed a warm personal concern. That was enough. Much to Holman's surprise, without his even mentioning the price he had offered or talking about the purchase of the crop, the grower said, "I can see you are being genuine with me, and you understand my position. I will accept your offer in the hope that things will improve soon for us both."

So get into the other person's boots. There's no better way to ease a difficult situation.

"We have a little carpet venture in China," says Adriana Bitter, president of Scalamandre Silks. "On the day of the Tiananmen Square massacre, when nothing was operating for big business, our little mill was. That day we sent off a telegram, saying we were terribly sorry they were suffering. We never mentioned the giant order that had to be delivered to England the following week. We thought, 'No way. Nothing's getting out.' But we received an answer, 'Thank you for your telegram. Your order was shipped this morning.' I don't know how they got it out of China, but they did. We have a good rapport with this little mill out in the mountains."

By seeing things from the mill workers' point of view, Bitter made sure the impossible order arrived.

This obsessive attention to customer service is a life-or-death issue in every business. At Harrison Conference

Services, Inc., if it means making the facilities more comfortable for women or serving a more healthful menu, no problem. Can do.

And it's not enough just to wait around for the suggestion box to fill up or the complaint letters to arrive in the mail. It's vital to stay one step ahead of the customers. Smart business leaders are always thinking about what the customer will want next—a few days, a few weeks, a few months from now. This is all part of thinking in terms of the other person's interests, a reversal of What's in it for me?

There's certainly no shortage of business publications being sold today—magazines, books, newsletters, on-line data services, fax reports—but the vast majority of these publications, Martin Edelston believed, were not delivering the practical information that many business people craved. "They're devoted to business news, more or less. But they don't tell you, in practical terms, how to deal with your employees, how to cut health costs. They'll talk about the healthcare problem, but they won't tell you how to dig into it." So Edelston started a company, Boardroom Reports, to fill that void.

Does it take a genius to dream up this stuff? Hardly. It takes leaders who are asking themselves day in and day out, "How does the customer rate our business? What will the customer want next?"

Just about every business can benefit from looking at the world this way.

"Last year," says SAS Airlines president Jan Carlzon, "each of our ten million customers came in contact with approximately five SAS employees. This contact lasted an average of fifteen seconds. These fifty million moments of truth are moments that ultimately determine whether SAS will succeed."

Looking at things from the other person's perspective doesn't happen on its own. The questions aren't complicated, but they have to be asked. Ask them at work, at home, in the social scene. You'll soon be seeing things as others do.

What life experiences does the other person bring to this interaction? What is the other person trying to achieve here? What is the other person trying to avoid? What other constituencies does the other person have to serve? What will it take for the other person to consider this encounter a success? The answers to these various questions will be different at different companies, although some themes will no doubt recur. But whatever the precise answers, the point here isn't simply to go along with everything the other person wants. It is to make a genuine, sincere effort to figure out what the other person is really looking for—and as much as is humanly possible, to deliver that. As Dale Carnegie said, "If you can help people solve their problems, the world is your oyster."

It took an angry complaint letter to remind Corning's David Luther that his idea of great isn't necessarily the customer's idea of great. Luther was working in Britain in those days. Corning had sent around a comprehensive customer survey, and this one respondent did not mince words. "Corning stinks," he wrote.

As any good executive would, Luther followed up on the complaint and invited the man in for a chat. "Well, why does Coming stink?" Luther asked the man, who worked in a warehouse that was stocked with Corning products.

"It's your labels," the man said.

"Ah, I got you," Luther said, brightening up. "You've got to be confusing us with somebody else. Our labels are printed by computer. They show the source of manufacturing, the country of origin, your code, our code, the date, everything you want to know."

The man shook his head slowly back and forth. "Son," he asked, "have you ever been in a warehouse?"

"Well, yeah," Luther answered. "I spent ten years in a warehouse, as a matter of fact."

"Have you ever been to my warehouse?" Luther admitted he hadn't. "Come with me," the man told him. So the two of them marched directly to the warehouse. The tiers in this particular warehouse were higher than those Luther was used to back home. The upper tiers, in fact, were way up above Luther's head.

The warehouse man directed his attention to one of the top shelves. "We put Corning stuff up there," the man said. "But can you read the labels up there?"

"No," Luther had to admit. "I can't, as a matter of fact."

"That's the point," the warehouse man told him."Can't see it." So that's what he meant by "Corning stinks." Luther learned a valuable lesson that day. "You've got to get inside the customer's organization," he said. "Think about the person in the warehouse. He's got requirements. She's got requirements." And you won't find out about them unless you bother to ask.

If you want to have more successful relationships with your customers, your family, and your friends, look at things from the other person's perspective.

STEP OUTSIDE YOURSELF TO DISCOVER WHAT'S IMPORTANT TO SOMEONE ELSE.

□

Chapter—6
Listening to Learn

I met a distinguished botanist at a dinner party given by a New York book publisher. I had never talked with a botanist before, and I found him fascinating. I literally sat on the edge of my chair and listened while he spoke of exotic plants and experiments in developing new forms of plant life and indoor gardens. I had a small indoor garden of my own, and he was good enough to tell me how to solve some of my problems.

As I said, we were at a dinner party. There must have been a dozen other guests. But I violated all the canons of courtesy, ignored everyone else and talked for hours to the botanist.

Midnight came. I said good night to everyone and departed. The botanist then turned to our host and paid me several flattering compliments. 1 was most stimulating, he said. I was this, and 1 was that. And he ended by saying I was a most interesting conversationalist.

An interesting conversationalist?

I had said hardly anything at all. I couldn't have said anything if I had wanted to without changing the subject, for I don't know any more about botany than I do about the anatomy of a penguin. But I had done this: I had listened intently. I had listened because I was genuinely interested. And he felt it. Naturally, that pleased him. That kind of listening is one of the highest compliments we can pay anyone. And so I had him thinking of me as a good conversationalist when in reality I had been merely a good listener and had encouraged him to talk.

—DALE CARNEGIE

There are two very good reasons to listen to other people. You learn things that way, and people respond to those who listen to them.

This point sounds so obvious it looks almost silly sitting there in cold, hard type. But it's a lesson that most of us spend most of our lives forgetting to apply.

Hugh Downs was lucky. The longtime host of ABC's 20/20 program found out about listening early in his broadcasting career. This was back in the days of radio, when Downs was just getting started as an on-air interviewer. He witnessed firsthand how a simple failure to listen could trip up one of his most experienced colleagues.

"He was interviewing a man who had escaped from a Kremlin prison in the thirties," Downs recalled. "This guest was telling him how, for months, the prisoners had been trying to tunnel their way out of there. They'd dug and dug. They'd eaten the dirt. They'd arranged to have a saw smuggled in. And when they figured their tunnel was outside the prison walls, they began digging up. It was quite a dramatic story.

"Then this one midnight, they were finally ready to break loose. They had already sawed through a wooden platform above their heads. But when this one prisoner stuck his head out, he was shocked by what he saw. 'When I got up,' he told the interviewer 'I realized I was right in the middle of Josef Stalin's office.'

"And do you know what this interviewer said next?" Downs asked, recalling that long-ago day. "Do you have any hobbies?"

Not "Are you serious? Josef Stalin's office?" Or "Stalin wasn't working late that night, I hope." Or "So tell me, were you tempted to plop down in the butcher's chair and light up one of his cigars?" Had the interviewer been listening at all, he would have known to ask any number of follow-up questions the members of his audience undoubtedly had on their minds. But the interviewer's attention was off somewhere else. All he could manage was that ridiculous non sequitur. And his listeners were deprived of the climax to a fascinating tale.

"That's a true story," Downs said. "And I've heard other interviews like that, where the interviewer just didn't listen. It's amazing what people can miss. It's a part of the business I call the yeah-well interview."

The importance of listening doesn't apply just to professional interviewers, of course. It is vital for anyone, anywhere, anytime, who hopes to communicate with others.

Listening is the single most important of all the communication skills. More important than stirring oratory. More important than a powerful voice. More important than the ability to speak multiple languages. More important even than a flair for the written word.

Good listening is truly where effective communication begins. It's surprising how few people really listen well, but successful leaders, more often than not, are the ones who have learned the value of listening.

"I don't sit on top of a mountain and get these visions of what we ought to do," says Richard C. Buetow, director of quality at Motorola, Inc. "I have to find out from other people. I have to do a lot of listening."

Even a great communicator like Buetow, who is expected to articulate and communicate the Motorola vision just about everywhere he goes, must also know when not to talk. In his words, "You have to be able to turn off your transmitter and listen—put the receiver on, let other people articulate ideas, and nurture them."

This understanding is a central part of Buetow's self-image as a business leader. He never talks about himself, for instance, as a grand strategist or a sophisticated corporate sage. He compares himself instead to a carrier pigeon.

"I don't solve one quality problem at Motorola," he explains. "If you ask me to do hardware, first thing I'll do is give you the telephone number of the person who is responsible for hardware. What I do is take the good ideas that I hear and carry them from place to place."

The underlying truth here is self-evident: No one can possibly know everything. Listening to others is the single best way to learn.

This means listening to employees, to customers, and to your friends and family—even to what harshest critics have to say. It doesn't mean becoming a captive of other people's opinions, but it does mean hearing them out.

You'll be thankful for many of their ideas.

Giorgio Maschietto, managing director of Lever Chile, S.A., the packaged-goods company, was responsible for running a string of factories in South America, including a giant Pepsodent toothpaste plant. The factory's production schedule was constantly being interrupted by the need to wash out the steel toothpaste tanks. One day one of the line operators made a suggestion, and Maschietto had the good sense to follow through.

"We were using just one tank," he recalls. "This line employee suggested we should put in a second tank. Now we can wash the first tank while using the second one, so there's no need to stop production anymore for tank washing. By adding a bolt in one case and by adding a small tank in another case, we've reduced changeover time by seventy percent and significantly increased productivity."

From the same source—the factory floor—Maschietto got a second toothpaste-production idea that was just as important. For years the factory had used a set of highly delicate and highly expensive scales beneath the toothpaste conveyer belt. Their purpose was to make sure each carton of toothpaste actually contained a tube. But the high-tech scales never quite worked. "Sometimes," Maschietto says, "we used to seal up empty cartons and send them out.

"One of the ideas of the men on the line was to replace all this expensive machinery and just put a small jet of airacross the conveyer belt where the tubes rolled by. The compressed air is regulated so that when the carton is empty, the pressure of the air is enough to throw the empty cartons off the belt."

Many people think of listening as passive, talking as active. Even the cliches people use in conversation— "sit back and listen"—hint at this pervasive misunderstanding of what true listening is about. Simply hearing what someone says is a relatively passive activity. But engaged, effective listening is a highly active sport.

Andres Navarro, president of SONDA, S.A., a South American computer-systems company, uses his native Spanish language to illustrate the difference between the two. "In Spanish," Navarro explains, "we have two words, oir and escuchar," the rough equivalent of "to hear" and "to listen." "To really listen is much more than just hearing. Many people, when they are hearing someone, they are really thinking to themselves, 'What will I answer?' instead of trying to listen to what the person is saying."

Active listening requires an intense involvement in a conversation, even when the listener's lips are still. That isn't always easy. It takes concentration. It requires genuine engagement. It calls for questioning and prodding. And it demands some kind of response, quick, thoughtful, on target, and concise.

There are many ways of displaying active involvement in a conversation, ways that don't entail jumping in and interrupting the other person's every seven words. The trick isn't to master every one of these techniques. Good listeners learn a few that they find comfortable and natural—and remember to put these few to work.

It can be an occasional nod, or an uh-huh, or an I see. Some people like to shift their postures or lean forward in the chair. At appropriate moments, others smile or shake their heads. Strong eye contact is another way of indicating to your conversation-mate, "Yes, I am listening closely to what you are telling me." And when the other person comes to a break in his or her talking, go ahead and ask a question that follows closely from what was just said.

What's important here isn't the precise listening technique that is chosen. None of these methods should ever be used in a wooden or rote way. These are just a few approaches that are worth being mindful of when the moment feels right. They will make the other person happier about speaking with you.

Elmer Wheeler was driving at much the same idea two generations ago when he wrote in his seminal book on salesmanship, Sell the Sizzle Not the Steak, "A good listener bends toward you physically. He leans on you mentally with every word that you utter. He is 'with you' every moment, nodding and smiling at the right times. He listens 'a little closer.'" This isn't good advice just for salesmen, Wheeler wrote. "It is a sound rule to follow for social and business success."

"A person who's actively listening," says Bill Makahilahila, Director of Human Resources at SGS-Thomson Microelectronics, Inc., "is usually the one who is asking questions and then waiting for a response, as opposed to coming up with an instant solution. Active listening is occurring when the employee feels and knows beyond a shadow of a doubt that you're not just jumping to conclusions."

Makahilahila thinks this is such an important concept that he has even created an Active Listening Award for SGS-Thomson supervisors who excel at listening. He has come up with a three-question test for determining whether someone is listening actively or not:

1. Do you ask questions and wait for an answer?
2. Do you respond quickly and directly to the questions that are asked?
3. Does the other person feel you are listening actively to him or her? Chris Conway, an insurance company marketing specialist living in Omaha, Nebraska, was a single parent raising two young boys. He learned how to really listen from his older son.

"Dan belongs to a group of about fifteen teenagers who meet weekly with an older couple just to discuss current issues and how the young people relate to them," Conway says. "The couple is there to facilitate the conversation. I asked Dan how he liked participating in the group."

The boy spoke in unusually enthusiastic tones. He said he could tell the leaders were genuinely interested in the group by the way they listened so closely to what the young people said.

"Dan, I listen to you," the father said.

"I know, Dad," the boy said. "But you are always making supper, washing dishes, or doing something else. All you ever say is yes, no, or 'I'll think about it.' You don't even listen to me. These people turn and face me and cup their chin in their hand and really listen."

For the next five weeks, Chris Conway focused on listening to his two sons. "While I heap the food on the boys' plates, I only put a couple of vegetables on mine. Whenever the boys speak, I set down my fork, turn to them and listen. The result is that I have lost fifteen pounds. And our suppers have gone from an average of eight minutes to forty-two minutes long."

A good listening environment—that's where listening begins. It's impossible to ever listen effectively when fear, anxiety, or nervousness is present. That's why good teachers always make sure their classrooms are comfortable, hospitable places.

"I know for myself that when I'm nervous about something, I don't listen as well," says kindergarten teacher Barbara Hammerman. "I'm concerned with my own being. If the children are tense and nervous in a classroom, they're not free to listen." William Savel, retired chairman of Baskin-Robbins, the worldwide ice-cream and yogurt retailer, was once sent to Japan by the Nestle Company to run marketing and sales.

"The first thing I did was to visit with a number of U.S. companies that had Japanese subsidiaries," he recalls. He learned to speak Japanese. He slept in Japanese hotels. He ate Japanese food. He did everything he could think of to surround himself with things Japanese.

"The important thing is to listen," Savel said, "to really listen before you go in and start shooting your mouth off and telling everybody how smart you are. You've got to learn how dumb you are first. You have to go in and get to know the people, interact with them, don't put yourself above anyone else. Get around, talk to everybody, listen very intently, and don't make up your mind too fast."

Simply put, People everywhere love to be listened to, and they almost always respond to others who listen to them. Listening is one of the best techniques we have for showing respect to someone else. It's an indication that we consider them important human beings. It's our way of saying, "What you think and do and believe is important to me."

Strangely enough, listening to someone else's opinions is often the best method of getting them around to your way of thinking. Dean Rusk, President Johnson's secretary of state, knew this from decades of negotiating with some of the world's most stubborn political leaders. "Listening is the way to persuade others with your ears." It's true; listening can be a tremendously powerful tool for convincing others to see the world the way that you do.

"The real key," says merchant banker Tom Saunders, of Saunders Karp & Company, "is getting to understand a person and what he values and how he wants to look at investments and whether or not you could honestly say our approach was right and compatible for him."

Saunders is in the business of advising big corporations about how to invest prodigious sums of money. His number-one technique? Listening to them. It all "goes back to listening," he says. "What was really on his mind? Why had he said no? What was the real reason behind it?

"I've had a twenty-five-year relationship with AT&T, which has just been extraordinary. I think it's all basically been due to listening."

Saunders goes on, "I can give you the best-looking brochure. I can throw up all these slides. But still I've got to find out what's in there that's interesting to that person. What's on this person's mind? What does he think about? How does he look at things?"

The first step to becoming a strong, active listener is understanding how important good listening is. The second step is wanting to learn. Finally, you have to practice those budding listening skills.

"I learned mine in not such a pleasant way," recalls Wolfgang R. Schmitt, chief executive officer of Rubbermaid Incorporated, the home-products giant. "I learned mine by going through a divorce when I was young. I was very career-centered. In the process of trying to avoid the divorce, we went to a counselor. That was really the first time I understood how crucial good listening is. Here was something that was important to me —my marriage—and

I wanted to try to retrieve it. That was the first time that somebody said to me some very straightforward things."

About listening? "Not just listening," Schmitt says, "but internalizing other people's feelings and thinking about them. Then being able to mirror them back, so you can demonstrate their importance to you."

At Motorola small teams of employees are always encouraged to come in with their ideas. And the company's top executives sit quietly and listen. "I've sat and listened to hundreds of teams tell me about all these issues and solutions and so on," Motorola's Richard Buetow says. And it is out of those hundreds of conversations that Motorola's future has been built.

Those kinds of small group-discussions —hosted by executives who mostly keep their mouths shut —are a tremendously valuable way to institutionalize corporate listening. At Analog Devices, Chairman Ray Stata has created a technique he calls the CNA Roundtable. Meetings are held regularly. Small groups of employees from throughout the company are invited to sit down for no-holds-barred discussions with Stata and other top Analog executives. The general theme is "creating a new Analog for the '90s," or CNA, the company's internal slogan these days.

"It's not just a matter of answering the questions people ask," Stata explains. "What I do after a certain amount of discussion is I'll say, 'Now what I'd like to do is go around the table and have each individual tell me, What are your particular concerns right now? What are your suggestions? Where are you coming from?' And I sit there and take copious notes.

"That's called listening," he says. "Afterwards, I write a memo that summarizes what I heard."

Joe Booker took a new job as the leader of a quality-improvement program at the Allegheny Ludlum

Corporation, an import-export company in the steel business. Quickly his enthusiasm turned to fear. "The program had been in existence at the company's largest plant for about eighteen months, with poor acceptance by the plant's nearly two thousand employees. Since participation was voluntary, how would I get the departments to realize the need for quality improvement? In many cases they were already successful in using their own techniques."

After some thought, Booker realized that what he needed to do was convince the employees that he was a competent team player who would be an asset to them. What this meant, he realized, was some hard-core listening. "I began to visit each one of the plant's six departments with the goal of understanding how individuals felt about their products' quality," he says. "I avoided arguments about the program and guided each conversation to hear how that individual was key to the progress of quality improvement. I was able to find allies in each of the departments and with their aid encourage others to get involved in the challenge to meet world-class quality.

"Today our plant has the highest union-represented involvement in any of the company's finishing facilities. People understand how the next operation or department is their customer. This is a direct result of good listening and communication among all employees."

David Luther at Corning has discovered exactly that same rule. "One of the first questions I ask when I look at a communication plan is, How long does it take before you see the word listen? Most of these plans are full of 'Let me tell you this' or 'Let me tell you that and the other thing.'"

At Corning, Luther developed a process for turning listening into a practical improvement tool. He explains how that process works. "We'll call over to a factory. I want two groups of fifteen people, and I want them for five hours. And we'll come in. Usually there's the union head, he has an assistant, and I have an assistant. One of the union people and I will take one group of fifteen. My assistant and the other union person will take the other fifteen. So we have two people in front of each group.

"We take them through a process. The first thing we say is, 'What's right about quality? Remember what it used to be like here ten years ago. Can you think about how quality is better now? Okay, let's put that on the wall.'

"Second part: 'What isn't right about quality? The only thing you can't complain about is your boss. Everything else is fair.' And we put that on the wall.

"Then we'll take that second list and condense it to ten or twelve issues. There's always a little overlap. We want to get rid of the overlap. 'Now we're going to vote. We've got twelve items here. You've each got three votes, and as I point to each of these twelve items here, if that's one of your more important quality issues, raise your hand.'

"As you go through the list of twelve, six don't get any votes at all, a couple will get a few votes, and maybe two will go right off the chart. So let's talk about those complaints. "Then you take the two groups. You put them back together. You bring in the plant management. You have a spokesperson for each group get up and say, 'Here's what my group said.' So the first group says, 'We don't understand what the plant manager thinks.'

And the second group gets up and says, 'The plant manager never communicates to us.' Even the dimmest plant manager will understand that he or she has got a major issue there and it's transparent. You can see the whole thing. It develops right there with his or her people. And there is no sending away questionnaires and rating them or coming back. I mean it's happened right before your eyes and you saw the coincidence. You know each of these teams did not know what the other team was saying. Now, we've done this maybe fifty times."

These are all wonderful techniques. Many others have been developed inside well-led companies. Remember, the same two basic principles underlie them all:

1. Listening is still the best way to learn.
2. People respond to those who will listen to them.

The simple truth of the matter is that people love being listened to. It's true in the business world. It's true at home. It's true of just about everyone we come across in life.

"The secret of influencing people lies not so much in being a good talker as in being a good listener," Dale Carnegie wrote. "Most people trying to win others to their way of thinking do too much talking themselves. Let the other people talk themselves out. They know more about their business or problems than you do. So ask them questions. Let them tell you a few things.

"If you disagree with them, you may be tempted to interrupt. But don't. It's dangerous. They won't pay attention to you while they still have a lot of ideas of theirs crying for expression. So listen patiently and with an open mind. Be sincere about it. Encourage them to express their ideas fully."

They will never forget. And you will learn a thing or two.

NOBODY IS MORE PERSUASIVE THAN A GOOD LISTNER

□

Chapter—7
Teaming Up for Tomorrow

Adolph Seltz of Philadelphia, a salesman in an automobile showroom and a student in one of my courses, suddenly found himself confronted with the necessity of injecting enthusiasm into a discouraged and disorganized group of automobile salespeople. Calling a sales meeting, he urged his people to tell him exactly what they expected of him. As they talked, he wrote their ideas on the blackboard. Then he said, "I'll give you all these qualities you expect from me. Now I want you to tell me what I have a right to expect from you."

The replies came fast: "Loyalty. Honesty. Initiative Optimism. Team work. Eight hours a day of enthusiastic work."

The meeting ended with a new courage, a new inspiration—one salesperson volunteered to work fourteen hours a day—and Mr. Seltz reported to me that the increase in sales was phenomenal.

"The people had made a sort of moral bargain with me," said Seltz, "and as long as I lived up to my part of the bargain, they were determined to live up to theirs. Consulting them about their wishes and desires was just the shot in the arm they needed."

—DALE CARNEGIE

It used to be that big organizations were shaped like pyramids. They had many workers on the bottom and layer after layer of supervisors and middle managers above. Each layer had more authority than the one beneath it. And this multilayered structure rose ever so neatly to a perfect, predictable point—where the CEO, the chairman, and the board of directors got to sit.

Was this the best way to organize a company, a hospital, a school? Almost no one ever bothered to ask. The old pyramid was as it always had been: solid, impressive, and seemingly impervious to change.

Now this might come as a surprise to some people, but the pyramids are tumbling down. It's as if the slaves of ancient Egypt decided to return, and they're carting away the stones. The new landscape may never be as flat as the sandy Sahara. But you can bet the future will be a whole lot more horizontal than the past.

All those rigid hierarchies, all those departmental lines, all those intricate chains of command —all of it stifled creative work. And who can afford that when the world is changing so fast?

"Look at what happened to the former USSR as a hierarchy," says Richard C. Bartlett, vice chairman of Mary Kay Corporation. "The same thing will probably happen to China because of hierarchy. It doesn't work for governments. It doesn't work for corporations either. The biggest corporations we've got in the United States didn't even notice the world coming down around their ears."

Clearly what's been needed is a structure that loosens up the old rigidity, that could let people do their creative best, that could fully develop the talent that's been lying dormant for years. In more and more well-led organizations, the answer is being found in teams. Increasingly often, people are being asked to work beyond their disciplines, outside their cultures, above and below their usual ranks.

"The modern organization cannot be an organization of boss and subordinate," argues business theorist Peter

Drucker, professor of management at the Claremont Graduate School in California. "It must be organized as a team." Andres Navarro, president of Chile's SONDA, S.A., agrees. "The Lone Ranger is no longer possible," Navarro observes. "A guy by himself inventing something alone—the world is too complicated for that. You need several people from different disciplines working together at the same time."

Small groups of people, recruited from throughout the organization, brought together for ongoing projects or for some specific, limited task —to design a new product, to reorganize a plant, to restructure a department, to figure out how to add momentum to a quality-improvement program. Fading are the old departmental rivalries. And fading are the automatic promotions, the seniority-based pay scales, and the other frustrating vestiges of the old pyramid.

In pyramid companies, the engineers spent all day cooped up with other engineers. Now an engineer might just as easily be thrown into a group of salespeople and told, "Help make this product more attractive to the customer." Or "Figure out how to build that part faster." Or "Use your engineering expertise to guide this marketing group around a technical glitch."

As a result of groupings like this, marketing is actually listening to engineering, and engineering is listening back. At many big companies this never, ever happened before. And now manufacturing, customer service, labor relations, and all the other far-flung departments are communicating too. At some progressive companies, these entire artificial divisions are even beginning to disappear.

As Drucker argues, the world is not made up of privates and drill sergeants anymore. "The army was organized by command-and-control, and business enterprise as well as most other institutions copied that model," he writes. "This is now rapidly changing. As more and more organizations become information' based, they are transforming themselves into soccer or tennis teams—that is, into responsibility-based organizations in which every member must act as a responsible decision-maker. All members have to see themselves as executives." Look at how Mary Kay Corporation is organized. "The Mary Kay organizational structure is a free form," says Vice Chairman Richard Bartlett. "I like to think of it almost as a molecular structure, where people can go right through any artificial barriers. They are not confined to a box. They can participate in a creative action team right across departmental lines. And in our view of the world —and this sounds trite to say, but a few people have jumped on the bandwagon since —the customer is right smack on top.

"But in the way we do business, right below her is our sales force. Our organization is very focused on how to support that sales force. At the bottom of the organizational chart is something that is referred to as an insignificant green dot.

"The first time I ever did a slide presentation on how to structure an organization, the artist put a green dot down there," Bartlett recalls. "I'm the insignificant green dot. My personal view of the world is that there is no need for a president or chairman unless he is dedicated to serving the needs of others and to providing resources to the people who are getting the job done."

"Organizations are actually restructuring," says Adele Scheele, whose articles on career-management issues appear regularly in American and Japanese business magazines. "What used to work no longer works. People expected there would be a set path, and there is no set path. So the more you believe in that, the less likely you are to be able to be flexible and begin to take advantage of opportunities that never come labeled. You want to always be open."

These flattened organizations are turning up in all kinds of surprising places, even in the educational world. "Management is becoming a lot flatter," observes Marc Horowitz, principal of Cantiague Elementary School in Jericho, New York. "And there's a real need to build teams, lead teams, and motivate people horizontally. In many cases it has to be done without title, without financial remuneration or incentive. It's the team's performance that's key." What this means in Horowitz's school is that students no longer work by themselves all day long in rows of wooden desks. They cooperate. They work in teams. They produce group projects. The students are expected to help each other. The teachers also work more cooperatively than they ever have before.

"Now it's 'How do we relate together and get results in the real world?'" Horowitz explains. "We're preparing students for the future. They really can't work in isolation anymore. They have to get involved in a team effort, and half of that battle is learning the social skills to encourage those in the group who aren't doing so well. They should never be allowed to feel less than worthy because they slip up or they do not have all the answers."

Three first-graders at Horowitz's school were involved in a group project one day. One of the children had the task of writing the word two on a piece of paper. But the child misspelled the word, writing it as tow. When a girl in the group pointed out the error, the boy felt bad for a moment. But then the little girl said, "Don't worry about it. I know you misspelled it. But that was a beautiful w, okay?" She even gave him a pat on the knee, and all three of the students got a good lesson in working cooperatively.

The Harvard business school marketing faculty recently conducted a teamwork experiment with the first-year graduate students. Instead of the usual midterm case-study exam, these students were divided at random into teams of four. Each team was given a business problem to solve— and twenty-four hours to come back with a written plan. The members of each team would get the same grade.

"Initially there was much criticism," says John Quelch, the Harvard business school professor. "Some students complained that individual grades would be adversely affected by the fact that they were thrown into a team with a group of people they wouldn't have selected to work with." The school's answer: Welcome to the real world.

In the end, the Harvard students came around. When the student newspaper surveyed the students after the experience, they expressed an overwhelming support for the new group-project midterm exam.

"The most significant level of learning," Quelch says, "was probably among students in those groups that did not perform like clockwork. There were some groups which experienced tremendous disagreements, and in retrospect, those were the students who learned the most out of the whole process."

Effective teamwork doesn't happen by magic. It takes a cooperative group of players, and it takes a talented coach. You can't simply throw a few individuals together—even a few highly talented individuals —and expect them to perform brilliantly.

That's why the National Basketball Association all-star game so often falls short of its hype. Sure, the game features many of the finest players in America, brought together on a single basketball court. Pound for pound, there is no more talented collection of guards, forwards, and centers anywhere. So why does this floor full of phenomenal talent so seldom produce a phenomenal game?

Too much ego. Too much time in the spotlight. Too many mornings on the sports page. When it comes to playing as part of a unit, these superstars often fail to measure up. The missing ingredient is team-work.

There is an art to building successful teams, and even a great coach can rarely mold a winner overnight. But anyone who expects to be a leader in the years to come had better master a few basic coaching techniques. They are as necessary in the business world as they are on the basketball court.

CREATE A SHARED SENSE OF PURPOSE.

People working together can accomplish tremendous things. What gives a team that special boost is the unified vision the individual members share.

The ideas, the creativity, the intelligent sparks will ultimately have to come from the group itself. But a strong leader is often needed to focus all that energy—to clarify the vision, to establish goals, to help everyone understand what the team is about, to show the team members how their accomplishments will impact upon the outside world. Ray Stata, chairman of Analog Devices Inc., says, "You've got to provide the environment, the corporate objective, and the encouragement so that people as individuals and as teams of individuals can feel that they're world-class, that they are better than any other team, and that there's recognition and feedback which acknowledges that."

MAKE THE GOALS TEAM GOALS.

Unless the whole team wins, no one wins. This concept is most familiar in the world of sports, but it's just as true for teams of any sort. Individual records are fine for the history books, but really they're an afterthought. What matters far more is the performance of the entire team.

"When you get people involved in this way and they feed off each other, it's contagious," says Rubbermaid's Wolfgang Schmitt. "It becomes a lot more like being a member of a sports team versus being in an assembly line. There's just a big difference in the energy level they bring into the work, the intensity."

That's why most good coaches —and most good leaders—speak so often in the first-person plural. "We need ..." "Our deadline ..." "The job before us..." Good leaders always emphasize how everyone's contribution fits in.

In business: "Together we have to get this new product smoothly to market." If the ad man does marvelous work but the packaging specialist fails, that's not success.

In sailing: "Together we have to get this boat through he storm." If the navigator can read the stars like a paperback novel but the skipper doesn't know the difference between starboard and port, that's not success.

In politics: "Together we have to win this election." If the candidate is a splendid orator but the advance staff can't get her to the speech, that's not success.

TREAT PEOPLE LIKE THE INDIVIDUALS THEY ARE.

When individuals come together as a team, their individuality doesn't suddenly evaporate. They still have different personalities. They still have different skills. They still have different hopes and fears. A talented leader will recognize those differences, appreciate them, and use them to the advantage of the team.

Individually— that's how Bela Karolyi, the internationally renowned gymnastics coach, prepared his students for the Olympic Games. "If I wasn't producing what he wanted," recalls Olympic gold medalist Mary Lou Retton, a star student of Karolyi's, "he would ignore me. I'd rather him yell at me, I swear." But Karolyi was smart enough to recognize that that approach was exactly what Retton needed.

"I would do a vault," she recalls. "I'd put my hands up, and then I'd turn around. He would be looking down at the next girl, who was ready to go. Oh, I wanted his attention so much. I wanted him to say, 'That was good, Mary Lou.' He would use that to get results out of me, and that would push me to make the correction, to get that praise."

Was Karolyi just a grouch? Not at all. With other students he took an entirely different tack. Retton will never forget the approach Karolyi used on teammate Julianne McNamara. "She has a much different personality than I do," Retton says. "She's much more timid, a little reserved. He would be very gentle with her. If she wasn't makingthat correction, he'd come and put her body where it needed to be and talk quietly to her. He was always much more gentle with her. That's how he got personal results.

"He treated each student differently, and I think that's very important.

MAKE EACH MEMBER RESPONSIBLE FOR THE TEAM PRODUCT.

People need to feel their contributions are important. Otherwise they'll devote less than complete attention to the tasks at hand.

Make the project belong to the team. Let as many decisions as possible bubble up from the group. Invite participation. Don't dictate solutions. Don't insist that things be done a certain way.

The Jaycraft Corporation had a problem. Its biggest customer had a giant order —and a delivery date that seemed impossible to meet. Doug Van Vechten, the company president, could have imposed a solution from the top.

But he knew better than to try. Instead, he asked a team of his employees to figure out what to do. "They came back to me and said, 'We can move some things around here and there, and we feel that we can do it, and let's take the job,'" Van Vechten remembers. Jaycraft took the job and met the customer's delivery demand.

SHARE THE GLORY, ACCEPT THE BLAME.

When the team does well and is recognized, it's the leader's responsibility to spread the benefits around. A public pat on the back, a bonus from the top, a write-up in the company magazine—whatever form that recognition takes, everyone should get a generous share of it. Denis Potvin, former captain of the New York Islanders hockey team, knew how to share the glory when his team won the Stanley Cup. But just in case he didn't, coach Al Arbour knew enough about team play to remind him. "Make sure you let the other guys carry the cup," the coach whispered into Potvin's ear, a few seconds after the final buzzer of the championship game.

"He came on the ice and rushed over to the pile" of celebrating Islanders, Potvin explains. "We're all congratulating each other. I turned, and Al was there. We both hugged one another. And it was there, in my ear, that he told me that.

"I was very impressed," Potvin recalls. "Here is a guy who is in total control of the team. He was still thinking about his players even though the Stanley Cup had just been won—his first time as a coach."

People always appreciate being included in praise. It encourages them to give their greatest efforts and makes them want to work again with the leader who guided them to this success. And this kind of gracious-ness has one other benefit: in the end the leader gets a big share of the credit anyway.

When it comes to criticism, be a smart leader and take exactly the opposite approach. Don't point the finger at others. Never raise public complaints about the "weak link" in the chain. Step forward and accept whatever complaints arrive. Then speak privately with the team members about how the results might be improved, and turn their attention to doing better next time.

TAKE EVERY OPPORTUNITY TO BUILD CONFIDENCE ON THE TEAM

A great leader will believe firmly in the team and will share that belief with every member.

That's a lesson kindergarten teacher Barbara Hammerman puts into action in her classroom, and it applies just as well in the factory or boardroom. "I try to build a class spirit within the room," she says. "To the children in my class, we are the best class, and there is a feeling that we don't want to disappoint the group—one for all and all for one—that we have certain standards that are set and reviewed and continuously reinforced through the year. The children understand these standards."

They aren't intimidated by them. "They just love living up to these standards because we're great," Hammerman said. "Who doesn't want to feel as if they're part of the wonderful group? When they get compliments from others, they can begin to see the progress they are making and changes in themselves. And they just feel wonderful about themselves."

BE INVOLVED, STAYINVOLVED.

In those old pyramid companies, it was easy for the boss to remain relatively aloof. After all, that army of minions was always hovering around, just waiting to distribute the boss's latest wisdom to the troops.

This approach doesn't fly in the new team-based world. The strong leader has to be involved and stay involved. Visualize the leader as the commander of a busy aircraft carrier, standing out on deck. Planes are coming in. Others are taking off. The ship has to stay on course and also be protected from attack. All these considerations have to be factored in together.

The leader really does have to be there. "You've got to have the experience, and you've got to listen," says Jack Gallagher, president of North Shore University Hospital in Manhasset, New York. "But after a while, if you get enough experience, if you work hard enough, if you're smart enough, if you do your homework, then you get a good feel for all these planes going up and down and for all the other things around you."

You can't always draw up a precise battle plan. "You've got to get an intuitive feel for it, and you've got to have antennae out, the antennae in the back of your head," Gallagher says. "Sure, there are too many things going on, and this is a very complex business. But you can develop that intuitive feel."

BE A MENTOR

It's the leader's job to develop the talents and strengthen the people on the team. This is true in the short term, as the team members deal with their assignment at hand. But it's also true long-term: the leaders must take a genuine responsibility for the lives and careers of the members of the team.

"How would you like to improve?" "Where do you want your career to go from here?" "What kinds of new responsibilities would you like to be taking on?" It's your job as leader to ask all those questions and to use whatever knowledge and experience you possess to help team members achieve those goals.

Reinforce the confidence you have in their abilities. Give them standards to live up to. Issue genuine compliments in public: "Sally has done a terrific job on this report." Send private notes: "That was a great comment you made today. You got us all focused where we needed to be." And remember, if they succeed, you succeed.

At Harvard University's Graduate School of Business Administration, new faculty members aren't just left to sink or swim.

"All seven or eight instructors teaching our introductory marketing course meet every week for four hours as a group to discuss the cases that are coming up and how best to teach those cases," says Professor John Quelch. "They also review how the cases went the previous week, what improvements need to be made, and so forth. In this way, newly recruited instructors can pick up teaching tips from our more experienced faculty." The senior faculty members also provide other kinds of support. Three or four times a semester, one of them sits in on a new instructor's class. They come to help, not to judge. "They're there very much in a coaching role," Quelch explains, "rather than to develop a report for a file that's going to determine your promotion. The goal is to enhance the effectiveness of the asset—the new faculty member— that we've invested in."

After class the senior faculty member might provide advice for both short- and long-term improvement. "What I would try to say to a new faculty member," Quelch continues, "is, 'Here are five things you can do the next time you teach that will have a positive impact on the way you're received by the class.' Suggestions might include, for example, something as seemingly trivial as writing larger on the blackboard. Or 'Make sure that you don't hang around the blackboard and direct the class from one area at the front of the room. Wander around the entire room and stand behind the students. Share the experience.'"

As Walter Lippmann wrote upon the death of Franklin Delano Roosevelt, "The final test of a leader is that he leaves behind him in other men the conviction and the will to carry on."

Follow these few simple techniques and watch how your team succeeds. The greatest reward a leader can achieve—the greatest legacy a leader can leave—is a group of talented, self-confident, and cooperative people, who are themselves ready to lead.

TEAM PLAYERS ARE THE LEADERS OF TOMORROW.

□

Chapter—8

Respecting the Dignity of Others

The Chrysler organization built a special car for Franklin Delano Roosevelt, who could not use a standard car because his legs were paralyzed. W. F. Chamberlain and a mechanic delivered it to the White House. I have in front of me a letter from Mr. Chamberlain relating his experiences.

"I taught President Roosevelt how to handle a car with a lot of unusual gadgets, but he taught me a lot about the fine art of handling people. When I called at the White House," Mr. Chamberlain writes, "the president was extremely pleasant and cheerful. He called me by name, made me feel very comfortable, and particularly impressed me with the fact that he was vitally interested in things I had to show him and tell him.

"The car was so designed that it could be operated entirely by hand. A crowd gathered around to look at the car, and he remarked, 7 think it is marvelous. All you have to do is to touch a button, and it moves away, and you can drive it without effort. I think it's grand. I don't know what makes it go. I'd love to have time to tear it down and see how it works.'

"When Roosevelt's friends and associates admired the machine, he said in their presence, 'Mr. Chamberlain, I certainly appreciate all the time and effort you have spent in developing this car. It is a mighty fine job' He

admired the radiator, the special rear-vision mirror and clock, the special spotlight, the kind of upholstery, the sitting position of the driver's seat, the special suitcases in the trunk with his monogram on each suitcase. In other words, he took notice of every detail to which he knew I had given considerable thought. He made a point of bringing these various pieces of equipment to the attention of Mrs. Roosevelt, Miss Perkins, the secretary of labor, and his secretary. He even brought the old White House porter into the picture by saying, 'George, you want to take particularly good care of the suitcases.'

"When the driving lesson was finished, the president turned to me and said: 'Well, Mr. Chamberlain, I've been keeping the Federal Reserve Board waiting thirty minutes. I guess I had better get back to work.'"

—DALE CARNEGIE

Don Monti was sixteen years old when his family received the devastating news: Don had leukemia and, the doctors guessed, about two weeks to live.

"We were in Don's room at the hospital," recalls his mother, Tita Monti. "This was right after he was diagnosed. We were very careful not to let him know that he had a fatal disease. We told Dr. Degnan not to say anything. We told the desk. We kept this pretense going."

That night Don's parents decided to ignore about fifteen of the hospital's rules and prepared their son a home-cooked meal right in his room. "He loved fettuccine Alfredo," his mother recalls. "We shut the door. We had this little can of Sterno. We were cooking fettuccine Alfredo for him. We hear a knock at the door and in walks Tom Degnan. I held my breath. I thought, 'Oh God, what is he going to say?' This is all foreign to me.

"Dr. Degnan looks and says, 'That's my favorite dish.' He sat down and we served him. We never had the feeling, 'Well, he's the doctor and we're the patients.'"

There were any number of things Dr. Degnan could have said when he walked into Don Monti's room. He could have said, "Didn't anyone tell you about hospital rules?"

He could have said, "Why are you cooking in the room?" He could have said, "Fettuccine Alfredo is definitely not on the hospital meal plan."

But Degnan had respect for the personal dignity of his patient and the patient's family. He never pulled rank once. He just sat down beside them and treated the Montis like human beings. The only way to form trusting relationships is to respect the dignity of others.

Burt Manning, the chairman of J. Walter Thompson Company, the giant Madison Avenue advertising firm, was invited not long ago to speak before an audience of young copywriters. These men and women, most in their twenties and early thirties, were just starting out in this highly competitive, often cutthroat business, so they were eager to learn a few tricks from an ad-world legend like Manning, who had lasted at the top for as long as many of them had been alive.

"Brains and talent and energy are merely the entry fee for the race," Manning told his bright-eyed audience that day. "You can't even get in without them."

But those talents aren't enough, not by a long shot. "To win, you need more," he said. "To win, you have to know the secret and live by it. It's that simple. What is this magical secret? It's this: Do unto others as you would have them do unto you."

That's right, the Golden Rule, right in the middle of Madison Avenue. Manning's reasoning did not hinge on religion, ethics, self-satisfaction, or the difference between right and wrong, although he told the young copywriters that those are all fine reasons for following his advice. But he gave them another one too: the Golden Rule delivers.

"Even if you are the least altruistic person in the world, even if you are purely devoted to your own self-interest, money, prestige, promotions," the veteran ad man said, "the surest way to get it all is to follow unswervingly the Golden Rule."

The president of the corporation, the teacher in the classroom, the clerk at the supermarket—they will all do better, go further, accomplish more, and feel better about themselves if they can just master that one simple, time-honored rule: Do unto others as you would have them do unto you. Or stated in a more modern fashion, show respect for others. They will show respect for you.

The world today is not just an old boys' club. It is a vastly more integrated, more diverse place than it was even a generation ago. Nowhere is that diversity more apparent than in the business world. Women, gays, people with disabilities, people from a wide array of racial and ethnic backgrounds—they're all a part of the equation today.

To succeed in that changed environment, it is absolutely essential to get along comfortably with everyone, whatever their background or culture may be. "Only fifteen or twenty percent of the people entering the work force in the twenty-first century are not going to be minorities, women, or immigrants," predicts James Houghton, chairman of Corning, Incorporated. "I mean, we're there. So unless you want to avail yourself of only fifteen percent of the talent out there, you'd better get diverse real quick."

The best way to begin respecting another culture—or anything else, for that matter—is to learn about it. That was one of the main things that drew die late Arthur Ashe to professional tennis. "I knew there was a lot of travel involved," he said. "That is really what I looked forward to. I wanted to go to those places. I wanted to see those things I'd only read about in the pages of National Geographic. I welcomed the opportunity to get to know them.

"Looking back on it now," Ashe said in an interview just before his death, "I rank that as one of my greatest sustained sets of recollections, the interactions I've had with a very wide variety of people from a lot of different cultures.

"You can look at traveling two ways," Ashe said. "You can have a very haughty attitude about your own culture. You go to other places and look condescendingly down at people who have come from civilizations many thousands of years older than yours. Maybe they're not as technologically advanced, and you think our system is better. The other way to look at it is to say, 'Yes, their physical condition and circumstances are not good. But boy, what a rich theological or a rich cultural heritage they have. They've been here ten thousand years, so they must know something. We've only been around two hundred years.' I much prefer the second approach."

Even nations that are next-door neighbors often view each other differently. These differences must be recognized, respected, and never condescended to. That's what Helmut Krings discovered moving back and forth between Germany and Switzerland. Krings, a German, is vice president for Central Europe at Sun Microsystems, a leading workstation manufacturer.

"I avoid comparisons," he says. "I try to avoid making any reference to Germany. What people hate most is if you are constantly saying what you do at home is right and suggesting that they're not doing things properly in their country."

All people want respect for their own culture and language. It's only natural. Melchior Wathelet, the deputy prime minister of Belgium, grew up in a French-speaking Belgian family. Early in his political career, Wathelet decided to bridge his nation's language gap by learning to speak Flemish, the other official language. This made him Belgium's first French-Belgian politician to become fluent in both national languages. He showed his respect for all the nation's people. He became a national symbol of unity, and his political career soared. He had learned to live with diversity.

So how do you live comfortably with diversity in the corporate boardroom, in the university, in the local sales office, in the nonprofit organization, in the government today? The first step is a basic one: Put yourself in the other person's place. Other people are living, breathing human beings just like you are. They have pressures at home. They want to succeed. They want to be treated with the same dignity, respect, and understanding that you do. What's important, says Thomas A. Doherty, the chairman of Fleet Bank, "is the way in which people are treated on a daily basis. People want to be treated and recognized as individuals. That was true when I first came into banking thirty years ago, and I think one hundred years from now it's still going to be true." And Doherty is clear about the reason: "Because we're all human beings."

What matters, says Doherty, is "treating people with respect. Small things like 'Good morning' and 'Thank you.' My own feeling is that it's the role of management to create an atmosphere where people can perform at their highest level." That atmosphere exists where people feel they're being respected and treated like individuals. It's absent where people feel they're just a number.

Most successful people have learned over the years that making others feel important is seldom accomplished by a single or even a few grand gestures. It's a process made up of many little touches.

Adriana Bitter at Scalamandre Silks has seen the power of this reality. Times were tough for the fabric industry in the late 1980s and early 1990s, but the company survived by pulling together with the employees. "Our people have been incredibly wonderful, working with us to get through this," explains Bitter. "I mean they've been fantastic and I think it comes back to closeness. If we didn't have this closeness, why should they give anything back to us? You know you have to give to someone if you're going to get back. Anyway, that's our philosophy."

How do you create that closeness? By showing respect and compassion and dignity to the people who work with you, by acknowledging that they're human beings who exist outside the work environment. At Bitter's company, that meant having the second-in-command gently correct a visiting speaker when he referred to the employees as mill workers instead of artisans. It meant Bitter's walking through the mill and talking to one of the designers about overcoming his fear of flying so he could take a planned vacation. It meant leaving the door to the president's office open and welcoming a bare-chested artisan when he needed to talk about problems in the dye house. It meant learning to peak Spanish to communicate better with the crew.

Fred Sievert of New York Life is in a very different Industry, but he knows some rules are the same. The little touches are everything in insurance too. In the insurance industry, the agents are the company. If the agents don't sell, pretty soon there is no company. It's that simple.

Years ago Sievert was working for Maccabee, the international insurance firm. When the company moved into a new office building that housed several other companies, Sievert wanted to be sure that the important personal touches didn't get lost in the shuffle. So his first stop at the new building was at the security desk. "I rounded up the people who worked at security, ten or twelve of them," Sievert remembers. "They didn't even know we were in the insurance business, other than the name of the company. I said, 'Hey, we've got some key agents in Detroit, and if you know that a person coming in here is an agent, I mean roll out the red carpet. Do whatever you have to. If you've got to walk the visitor up to the seventh floor to find the right person, do it.' I later got great feedback from some agents about the way they were treated when they walked in the building."

All these little touches add up to one very big whole: people feeling good about themselves. People who believe their organization cares about them and understands their needs are the people who are likely to respond by working hard and trying to advance the organization's goals.

Dale Carnegie used to tell the story of Jim Farley, Franklin Delano Roosevelt's campaign manager. Farley made it his business to remember —and use —the names of everyone he came into contact with. Often this meant remembering literally thousands of names. While running Roosevelt's reelection campaign, Farley would travel by boat, train, and automobile, hopping from town to town, meeting hundreds of people at each stop. When he returned home after weeks on the road, he was exhausted. But he didn't rest before he had completed one task he considered absolutely essential: he'd send a personally signed letter to all the people he'd met on the campaign trail. And he'd start each letter with the person's first name: Dear Bill or Dear Rita.

Do people today still respond to those small things? You bet they do. Returning a phone call, remembering a name, treating someone respectfully—those are just about the most important things any leader can do. These basics, says ad man Burt Manning, "are what works. That's how people separate themselves from the crowd, from the masses, by doing these basic things and never stopping."

On a recent trip to Manning's office, a visitor was struck by a small gesture. There was only one hanger in the office. Manning took the visitor's coat and hung it on the hanger. He tossed his own coat over a doorknob. Trivial? Maybe, but don't think it wasn't noticed. Those are the little touches that send a message: "I care about you. Your concerns are my concerns. We are in this together." A real positive environment can be created that way.

And there is no better way of reinforcing it than by following the second step to the Golden Rule: Treat employees like colleagues, and don't condescend, dictate, or berate. They are your coworkers, after all, not your servants or your best friends. So treat them accordingly. Recognize the humanity that everyone in the organization shares. Playing the big boss doesn't motivate people to do anything but resent the individual who's pulling rank.

Given the great power of respect, why do so many managers fall into the habit of demeaning and yelling at the people who work for them? Often the reason is low self-esteem. "Managers are exposed," says John B. Robinson, Jr., executive vice president of Fleet Financial Group Inc., Fleet Bank's parent. "They're on the line. I've often seen people—because it's a difficult situation—adopt an unnatural style. I'm thinking of some people I've seen over the years who tried to be tough managers and yet they aren't really tough managers. It's a cover maybe because of their own discomfort." Does it work? Almost never. "They tend to abuse people verbally and try to demand respect by ordering people around or by being arbitrary or that sort of thing," Robinson explains, "and that's usually exactly counterproductive." The reason is simple: people rarely respond well to intimidation.

It's much more effective to let your employees see that you are a human being too. Treat people like equals, like valuable assets, not like another piece of the company's machinery. What has to be done, says Bill Makahilabila of SGS-Thomson Microelectronics, Inc., is "to strip ourselves from position, strip ourselves from title in terms of how we viewed it in the past. View it as everyone contributing."

For some business leaders this means a whole new understanding of the relationship between employee and boss. The right tone must be set for respect and open communication to occur. John Robinson believes, "I guess one of the things that you need to do is maintain a sense of humility. It's so easy in the corporate world, the higher we get, to really believe that we're as important as our title suggests or that we're as smart as our position says." Years ago Robinson found a great way to remind himself that, despite the fancy titles he has had, he's just like everyone else he works with. "I was the president of a bank when I was in my early thirties, and I'd feel very important about that," he recalls. "Then I'd come home and the baby would be wet and miserable, and I'd be changing the baby's diaper. Immediately it brought me back and gave me perspective. My kids are really what kept me in balance."

Put yourself in the other person's place. Don't condescend. Those are both important. The third step to the Golden Rule: Engage people. Challenge them. Invite their input. Encourage their cooperation.

Work, in most cases, is as big a part of their lives as it is of yours. Almost certainly they want to be involved. They want to be engaged. They want to be challenged and stretched. They don't want their opinions ignored.

People who are passionate and involved with what they do will do it well. As Ray Stata of Analog Devices Inc. puts it, "What people want is a feeling of importance, a feeling of impact, a feeling of influence."

How can this feeling be created? By empowering your employees, challenging them, involving them in the planning of your organization. Says Stata, "I think that the most important thing is that people have job assignments and tasks to do that they feel are commensurate with their ability or maybe stretch them somewhat beyond their ability. I think the most important part of motivation is to try to link the task to the individual in such a way that it is a real challenge, that there is a stretch of expectation."

Rubbermaid figured this out early. That company radically pioneered the employee empowerment method of management. When Rubbermaid had to design a multimillion-dollar piece of new equipment in the late 1980s, the bosses didn't rule the day. Instead Rubbermaid had the employees, the people who actually would be using the machine, lead the process. Wolfgang Schmitt explains, "We put together a team of six people. These were all production associates with one management associate. They went out to the various companies who make these kinds of equipment and did the benchmarking. They were the ones who made the recommendation on what to buy. They were the ones who went over and trained in Europe, in this case in Germany, on the machines. They came back with the supplier's people and set it up. They managed it. They scheduled it. They ensured the quality of it. They did the preventive maintenance."

The results of this approach for Rubbermaid have been profound. The company has one of the highest employee-retention rates in the business, and Rubbermaid employees work. From 1982 to 1992 Rubbermaid paid an average annual rate of return to investors of 25.7 percent.

Bill Makahilahila describes the process of empowering his employees as one of his most important roles. It's often a difficult one. It involves instilling a sense of confidence in employees, "helping employees process their own thoughts and their own ideas and then solidifying that in their minds so they can feel self-confident in carrying out and executing their skills," as Makahilahila puts it. It involves hanging back, supporting the decisions, not taking over.

"In my mind there is no such thing as a right or wrong decision," he says. "I need to give you the full authority to make the decision. Now, if it's not the best decision that has been made, we'll discuss it. But if it is the best decision, I'll reinforce it to you and help you recognize it."

It's difficult, but the results justify the effort. Employees become committed to what they're doing. Perhaps Ray Stata says it best: "I think the pinnacle of what's important, particularly for educated, professional, knowledgeable workers, is the whole issue of self-actualization, self-fulfillment. So the notion of continuing improvement and growth in the development of their capabilities is at the end of the day the most important thing to motivate people."

Treat people well, treat them like equals, and engage them in the team process of work. There is one final way to create the workplace of dignity: Humanize the organization in ways big and small.

Symbolic efforts can play a big role here. For instance, get out from behind that big executive desk. Joyce Harvey of Harmon Associates Corporation has a small conference table in her office, and she uses it. "We sit around and talk," Harvey says. "I very often have a midday meeting, and I always make it a habit to bring lunch for any employee who's staying through the lunch hour. It makes it more casual and more informal, and it shows that we care and respect their time."

E. Martin Gibson, chairman of Corning Lab Services Inc., moves beyond symbolism. He thinks that humanizing an organization is so important that he's even structured the physical plants of his facilities with that in mind. "I think employees working in a single location with ten, fifteen, twenty thousand people is a disaster," says Gibson. "I mean I can't imagine myself getting out of the car and walking through a parking lot with ten thousand people in a huge complex. I would always ask myself the question, 'If I vaporized, would anyone even know it?' Chances are no. Or all they would say is, 'Where's old what's-his-name?'"

A worker who feels this disassociated isn't going to be very committed to an organization. Corning Lab Services, knowing this, has come up with a solution. The company has thirty-two different physical locations. While one of them is large—nineteen hundred employees—the rest range between three hundred and six hundred employees.

The results? "We've got people who, when they go to work every morning, know each other's names," said Gibson. "If they vaporized, someone would know. You know people would miss you because you're working in a small unit. Everyone knows your first name. It's exciting." Wolfgang Schmitt of Rubbermaid agrees. That's why he tries to keep his facilities in the four-to-six-hundred-employee range. Why that size? To save money? Not really. "What we think is really crucial is the people relationships," explains Schmitt. "When you get beyond the four- to six-hundred number, we think the personalized aspect of that relationship, the understanding, the empathy goes away. You start having to layer in overhead to artificially create understanding rather than having it sort of organically present. So both from a humanistic viewpoint and from a pure cost viewpoint, it's just as prudent, really smart, to stay in these units that are about that size."

Schmitt reached that conclusion when interviews with employees revealed that that size pleased the employees. "We find that the more we stick with that mode, the more people feel good about being a part of the organization, the more connectedness there is."

These issues are vitally important, and they aren't just for top managers. All of us—at whatever position —will go further and accomplish more by respecting the importance and the dignity of others, whatever their position, background, or relationship to us.

This is not a new concept. Years ago Dale Carnegie was applying it to people all over the world. "Do you feel that you are superior to the Japanese?" Carnegie asked. "The truth is that the Japanese consider themselves far superior to you. Do you consider yourselves superior to the Hindus in India? That is your privilege. But a million Hindus feel infinitely superior to you.

"Each nation feels superior to other nations. That breeds patriotism and wars.

"The unvarnished truth is almost all the people you meet feel superior to you in some way. And a sure way to their hearts is let them realize in some subtle way that you recognize their importance in the world and recognize it sincerely."

TRULY RESPECTING OTHERS IS THE BEDROCK OF MOTIVATION.

□

Chapter—9

Recognition, Praise, and Rewards

In the early nineteenth century, a young man in London aspired to be a writer. But everything seemed to be against him. He had never been able to attend school more than four years. His father had been thrown in jail because he couldn't pay his debts, and this young man often knew the pangs of hunger. Finally he got a job pasting labels on bottles in a rat-infested warehouse, and he slept at night in a dismal attic room with two other boys—guttersnipes from the slums of London. He had so little confidence in his ability to write that he sneaked out and mailed his first manuscript in the dead of night so nobody would laugh at him. Story after story was refused. Finally the great day came when one was accepted. True, he wasn't paid for it, but one editor had praised him. One editor had given him recognition. He was so thrilled that he wandered aimlessly around the streets with tears rolling down his cheeks.

The praise, the recognition that he received through getting one story in print changed his whole life. If it hadn't been for that encouragement, he might have spent his entire life working in rat-infested factories. You may have heard of that boy. His name is Charles Dickens.

—DALE CARNEGIE

Mary Kay Ash, the cosmetics-company founder, began her life in the business world by giving sales parties for the Stanley Home Products Company. She wasn't a very good saleswoman—not at first. "We had to give the hostess a four-dollar-and-ninety-nine-cent mop and duster," Ash recalls. "I was making about seven dollars a party, so when I walked out the door, that left maybe two bucks." But Ash had three small children to support and not many marketable skills. So she kept on plugging.

After a few weeks she realized she wasn't going to make a living this way, not unless something changed, fast. The time for drastic action had arrived. "I watched all these people telling me what they sold, and I said, 'How did they do it? Gee whiz, nobody bought those mops from me.' I didn't know how to do it. So I said, 'I've got to go to the Stanley convention. I've got to find out how to do it because I've got three kids to support.'"

For a single mother in Texas in those days, that was a real gamble. Ash had no money and no encouragement. "I had to borrow the money that it took to go to the convention," she said. "It cost twelve dollars. That included the chartered train—now you're going to know how long ago this was—from Houston to Dallas and back again, and it included three nights at the Adolph us Hotel. You couldn't step across that threshold today for twelve dollars. I borrowed the twelve dollars from a friend. I lost a lot of friends asking for the twelve bucks. I just tried to borrow it, and the one I got it from said, 'You ought to be staying home buying shoes for your kids with twelve dollars. You ought not to be going on those wicked things that men go to.'"

But Ash wasn't swayed. "They didn't mention eating, and I liked to eat. So I thought, 'Gee whiz, I better pack some cheese and crackers.' So I packed a pound of cheese and a box of crackers and emptied out my Stanley samples suitcase. It was the only suitcase I had. I didn't have a real suitcase. And I put my only other dress in it, along with the cheese and crackers. "I got on that train, and people began to sing, S-T-A-N-L-E-Y, Stanley all the time. That's the slogan you will hear, nothing buzzing in your ear.' And I was like, 'Oh, my gosh,' I was so embarrassed. "Those crazy people.' I pretended not to be one of them. I didn't have any clothes, I didn't have anything. I must have looked pretty awful, but I got there and that changed my life."

Changed her life?

"The Stanley people crowned a girl queen. Her name was Livita O'Brien. I'll never forget, she was tall and skinny and black-haired and successful. My exact opposite. I watched from the last row in the back of that room, and I decided next year I was going to be the queen. They gave her an alligator bag. That was the biggest award. I wanted it with all my soul. I wanted that alligator bag.

"They didn't have a manual on how to sell, but they said three things. First, get a railroad track to run on. Then, hitch your wagon to a star. Well, I had my work at Stanley, and I hitched my wagon to that woman's star so hard she must have felt it from the back row. Finally they said, tell somebody what you're going to do. Well, I looked around the room. I decided no use telling any of them. I'd go up to the president, who was standing at the front. I went up to Mr. Frank Sammy Beverage, and I said, 'Mr. Beverage, next year I'm going to be the queen.'

"Now, if he knew who he was talking to he would have laughed. I was three weeks in the business, seven-dollar Stanley-party average, and I was going to be queen next year? Come on now, really. But he was a very kind man. I don't know what he saw in me, but he took my hand, looked me straight in the eye, and said, 'You know, somehow I think you will.' Those seven words changed my life. I couldn't let him down. I mean I had pledged that I would be the queen next year." And she was.

Mary Kay Ash went on to found a highly successful cosmetics company, using part-time Mary Kay representatives to sell products to their friends, neighbors, and coworkers. She was motivated to succeed before sheever joined Stanley. She had to be: she had no husband, no other job, and three hungry children at home. Plus, she wanted the good feelings that come with being a success. The encouragement she got from the president of the Stanley company gave her the incentive she needed: a boost to her self-esteem, a feeling that someone else in the world cared if she succeeded.

Sometimes motivating people can truly be that simple.

All people, from the president of the most successful corporation to the clerk at the supermarket bottle return, want to be told that they're doing a first-rate job, that they're smart, they're capable, and their efforts are recognized. A little bit of recognition —a dash of encouragement at just the right moment—is often all it takes to transform a good employee into a great one.

"Why," asked Dale Carnegie, "don't we use the same common sense when trying to change people that we use when trying to change dogs? Why don't we use meat instead of a whip? Why don't we use praise instead of condemnation? Let's praise even the slightest improvement. That inspires the other fellow to keep on improving."

It's not complicated at all. But for some reason many people find it hard to distribute even well-deserved praise. "I used to find it difficult to give feedback, either positive or negative, and I don't know why," New York Life's Fred Sievert says. "It's so simple, and the value it brings is unbelievable. I don't know why I ever resisted stopping and saying, 'You know, I really appreciate you. Thank you for what you've done. I know you've put in a lot of extra time, and believe me, I see it.'"

After years of holding back, Sievert said he finally learned the importance of giving praise, in part from the man who was his boss. "He's a remarkable person, and he gives daily feedback," Sievert says. "He'll tell you when he's got a problem or something negative on his mind, but he'll also say, 'I appreciate you, and what you're doing is terrific' It's so reassuring to hear that." The comments don't have to be earth-shatteringly large. "Occasionally," Sievert goes on, "he recognizes I'm working too hard, and he'll say 'Get out of here. Go home. Spend time with your family. Take some vacation days.' Just the fact that he sees it is of great value to me."

Rewards. When that word is used in the business world these days, it is almost always a euphemism for money. Salary, bonuses, benefits, perks —those are the kinds of rewards most people think about, the financial kind.

Now, there's no denying that money matters. In our society, it matters a great deal. But the full truth of the matter is that money is only one of the reasons most people go to work in the morning and only one of the things they bring home with them at night. Protest as we will, even the most materialistic among us care intensely about other kinds of rewards.

Two items are at the very top of the reward list: self-respect and the respect of others. Those are two of the most powerful motivating forces around. "People love to look good," Harrison Conference Services' Walter Green is constantly reminding himself. "So part of what you want to do is to create an environment for people to look good."

That's what James Houghton has done at Corning. He tries to create an environment where employees can look good and feel good. That's a recipe of a thousand ingredients, but one of them involves Corning's procedure for dealing with employee suggestions.

Before becoming involved in the quality process, Corning used to solicit employees' advice in a half-hearted way. A few suggestion boxes were stuck off in the corners of Corning factories and offices, where mostly they sat gathering dust. Recalls Houghton, "Our suggestion system was like everybody else's in the sense that if you put it in there, and if it was accepted, you might get some money for it. But what would happen is that you would put in the suggestion, and the suggestion box was really just a black hole. You would hear nothing. Maybe six months later you would hear something. And once you heard something, you would be mad. Either you would be told you wouldn't get any money, or you'd get some money and you'd think it wasn't enough. Not only would you be mad, but everybody else around you would be mad because you got the money and they didn't."

Today Corning handles employee suggestions far differently. "Now the boxes are gone," along with the whole approach they represent. "Not by mandate. Place by place, they just disappeared."

That's not all that's changed. There's no money awarded in Coming's current employee-suggestion program, but there is recognition. "What people get is Employee of the Week. They get their picture up on the board, or they get flowers or a coffee mug, or somebody just says thank you." That acknowledgment is what makes the program work.

Don't employees miss the money? Not so you'd notice, Houghton says. "We set up only one rule. If a suggestion is made, there has to be an answer within a couple of weeks* It depends, a week or two weeks, whatever, but there has to be a quick answer. Yes or no or we're thinking about it."

But now that money has been taken out of the equation, the number of suggestions has fallen, right? "Last year," Houghton reveals, "I think we got eighty times as many suggestions as we ever got. We implemented around forty or fifty times as many."

People participate for several reasons. They want to improve the quality of their work lives—that's obviously part of it—and they make suggestions because they know that someone will listen when they do. But just as certainly, they participate because they want the self-respect and the public acknowledgment that come with submitting a good idea. Houghton says he wasn't the slightest bit surprised. "What it says to me is that people care, and they want to be involved. All you have to do is release them and say thank you. It's amazing what happens."

Houghton's right. Employees who feel that their contributions are being recognized and respected do accomplish amazing things. Making employees feel appreciated, focusing attention on their good ideas, inviting them to attend trade shows that used to be limited just to the top brass, saying, "Thank you. We know you're a good employee. We value you and your work"—that is the beginning of effective motivation.

Well-led companies today are spending time, energy, and money bringing these nonmonetary rewards to life.

"What I'm doing now," said Anders Bjorsell, president of Elektrotryck AB, Sweden's largest producer of printed computer cards, "is giving recognition in front of the whole group. That's very important—to tell someone in front of as many people as possible, 'Hey, you did a very good job.' It's not nearly as good to say that privately."

The pleasure comes from receiving recognition publicly. "That's what makes people feel appreciated," Bjorsell believes. "You should never stop doing this, and you can never do it enough."

Val Christiansen owns the highest-volume Denny's restaurant in America. That's number one out of eighteen hundred nationwide.

Christiansen's restaurant, which is located in Victorville, California, in the high desert between Los Angeles and Las Vegas, serves lots of salads, soups, sandwiches, and main courses. But Christiansen had noticed one area of weakness. Too many of the customers finished with their meals and then called out for the check. What the restaurant needed, Christiansen decided, was to sell more pies. So he announced a contest to see who could sell the most.

"When we started," he recalls, "we were selling two pies a day. So I explained to the crew how I thought they should sell pies. I gave them a little demo on how to sell pies. That crew knows me well enough now to say, 'Okay, Mr. C, if we start selling all these pies, what's in it for us?' I mean they are a bunch of ruthless capitalists, and we understand that, and that's okay."

The top seller on each shift, Christiansen told the employees, would be treated to a big night on the town. "That person and their spouse or whoever will be driven into Los Angeles in a chauffeured limousine to see Phantom of the Opera."

The day-shift winner, a woman who had never seen a play before, brought her husband along for the big night. "They spent the night in this huge stretch limo. They had a wonderful time. That was Friday night. Sunday morning, I come in. She catches me at the cash register. She's in uniform, working. She puts her arms around me. She doesn't hug me. She holds me, and holds and holds."

"Some opera, huh?" Christiansen asked her.

He recalls the scene. "We're busy. We're jumping. The place is packed with people. And she's just holding me. She releases me, and the tears are just coming down her face. She says to me, 'Mr. C, I love you. Thank you.' She says to me that she's giving me notice. She'll quit in thirty years."

All because of that one act of recognition.

"It built her self-esteem," Christiansen says. "Our pies went from two a day to seventy-one pies sold a day. So I got rewarded economically, and I got rewarded emotionally. I can't throw money at an employee and expect to get those kinds of results."

There is no shortage of reward programs out there to copy —almost as many as there are well-led companies today. Some of these programs are quite imaginative. The possibilities are limited only by the creativity of the people running them. So give the people at SGS-Thomson credit. They are one creative group.

They started an unusual award program called the Human Resource Quality Award, where employees are recognized for excellence, not in manufacturing or research and development or production, but in human relations. Bill Makahilahila, Director of Human Resources, describes the program he created. "We have four awards that we give out every quarter to managers who demonstrate certain behaviors. One is called the Golden Ear Award, and we actually have an award with a golden ear stuck on a plaque. It's for demonstrating good listening skills. Employees can nominate a manager or another employee or whoever it may be who demonstrates these skills. Then we have the Silver Tongue Award. The Silver Tongue Award has to do with effective communication, and not just in formal presentations. We have this unique plaque that the winner gets, and it's got a silver tongue coming out. We thought we'd make the system a little humorous using various body parts."

No, there is no Big Feet Up on the Desk Award.

"We have the Empowerment Award," Makahilahila continues. "That's for demonstrating to employees how we empower one another. And we have the fourth award, which is the major award. It's called the People Leadership Award. This is for the person who demonstrates all of the best characteristics —honesty, integrity, sincerity —on a regular basis. This person should also demonstrate effective communication, listening skills, interpersonal skills, people skills, and so forth. Now, this particular award plaque shows a leader holding his or her people up on a platform. So the whole concept here is actually supporting and holding up people as opposed to looking down on them."

Then there's Mary Kay Cosmetics Inc. That company has no equal in the contest for the most striking reward. At Mary Kay the top earners of the year receive a pink—yes, a pink—Cadillac. "About three years after we started, we were doing fairly well," Mary Kay Ash explains. "We had gotten to a million dollars, as a matter of fact. I needed a new car, so I went down to the Cadillac dealer, and I took my little compact out of my purse. I said to the man, 'I want a new Cadillac, and I want it painted this color.'"

The salesman got a pale look on his face. "He looked at it, and he said, 'Oh, Mary Kay, you don't really. Really, you don't. Let me tell you what it's going to cost you to get that thing repainted when it gets here and you don't like it.' I said, 'Please, I want it pink.' He said, 'Okay, but don't forget I warned you. Don't blame me for this disaster.'

"It came, and even on the way home it created a sensation with people driving by. It was amazing. It really was. You know how you can sit in a black Lincoln at a stop sign two hours and nobody will let you through? Drive a pink Cadillac. It's amazing the respect and admiration that thing gets."

Memorable? Yes. Understated? No. But then no one ever accused Mary Kay Ash of being understated.

"So the people loved it. They saw it as a big pink trophy on wheels, and they wanted to know, What do we have to do to get one?" She said. "My son Richard is the financial wizard of the company, and I took the question to him. I said, 'Richard, put a pencil to this, and tell me what someone would have to do to be able to win a pink Cadillac' He said, 'Oh, Mother, really,' but he figured it out. He told us how much. And you know the higher you put the thing, the higher they'll jump. So the first year we gave one. Second year, five.

Third year, ten. Fourth year, twenty. After that, we opened it up to anybody who does a certain number of dollars, and that's the way it remains today.

"So today we have sixty-five million dollars' worth of cars running around the nation, and even if you don't know anything else about Mary Kay Cosmetics, if you see a pink car in Salem, Massachusetts, it's Mary Kay. People know that. It's become a symbol." A useful symbol for the company and a useful symbol for the employees as well. It says, "You're superior. You've done a topflight job. Keep it up."

The United States Government isn't passing out pink Cadillacs. Not yet, at least. But even the government has gotten into the act when it comes to creative recognition. It's set up the Federal Quality Institute.

The Institute was founded in 1988 by an order of President Reagan. Its original mission was to try to find ways for increasing productivity in government. The think tank that was hired to do the initial research and planning on the idea reached the same conclusion that businesses like Corning and Motorola had: if you want to increase productivity, focus positive attention on quality and keep it there. Productivity will follow. "People are the most important part of the equation," says G. Curt Jones, the institute's senior quality executive.

As an integral part of Washington's quality-improvement plans, the institute began its own program of employee recognition, the President's Award. This is the public-sector version of the Baldrige Award, and believe it or not, the competition is just as stiff. One year's award went to the IRS service center in Ogden, Utah, whose employees figured out how to process tax returns more quickly, even in the face of i severe budget cuts.

Awards like this are just one idea. American Airlines has found an exquisitely targeted method for rewarding its employees. The airline's customers are brought directly into the process. Since flight attendants do most of their work in the air, literally thousands of miles away from supervisors, it's difficult for the airline to know exactly who is and who isn't doing a stand-out job. Given the constraints of a union contract, the airline is limited in its ability to pay certain flight attendants more than others.

But American Chairman Robert L. Crandall came up with a creative way around these problems. Gold-and platinum-level members of American's frequent-flyer club receive special certificates that can be turned over to a flight attendant in recognition of exemplary service. The flight attendants can cash in the certificates for free trips and other benefits. It's a creative method that works for the customer, who gets the pleasure of expressing thanks in a concrete way, and it works for the flight attendants too.

This idea of using rewards and recognition as an integral part of doing business isn't a new one. It's as old as the personal thank-you note.

John Robinson of Fleet Financial Group, Inc., learned that from an old friend several decades ago. "Jim Bender was a very successful salesman early in his career, and he told me what he used to do was he'd go on the road and make calls all day long. Then he'd go to his motel room at night and set out a bottle of bourbon and have a stack ofpaper. He'd always write a personal note.

"Throughout his life he's written, handwritten, all these personal notes," Robinson says. "And in this age of very sophisticated marketing and direct-mail marketing and that sort of thing, nothing has quite the impact of a hand-scribbled note saying, 'Gee, you did a great job handling that situation,' or 'I really admire how you handled so and so.

Do people care about these small acknowledgments? Joyce Harvey of Harmon Associates Corporation sure thinks so. "We have little notes that are printed to say, 'Thank you. We appreciate what you did today.' I find that as I go around the office, they're tacked up over people's desks. I used to find that people were helping each other and never getting recognition for it from their colleagues. Now they get a simple 'Thank you' or 'I appreciate what you did' or 'You made my life a little easier.' It's working very well."

Reward, recognition, praise. It doesn't matter how you do it; what matters is that you do it, again and again and again. The bottom line on rewarding employees is this. Sure, money's wonderful. But it's not the only effective reward. If you have money to spend, use it intelligently. Reward excellence. Encourage employee participation. Spend it in ways people appreciate.

And whether your budget is small or large, follow the advice of writer and lecturer Florence Littauer. Littauer was asked unexpectedly one day to give the children's sermon at her church. One passage from the Bible came to mind, but it was a difficult one for children to grasp: "Let no corrupt communication proceed out of your mouth but that which is good. Good to the use of edifying that it may minister grace unto the hearers."

Littauer worked with the children, deciphering the difficult words, and finally came up with an interpretation that she felt captured the meaning of the passage: "Our words really should be like a present," she said, and the children seemed to agree. "A little gift. Something that we give to other people. Something that they want. Something that they reach out for. They grab our words, and they take them in, and they love them. Because our words made them feel so good."

Littauer went on like that a bit, comparing words to gifts. Then she summed up her message. "Now," she said, "let's start from the beginning. My words should not be bad. They should be good. They should be used to build up, not knock down. They should be words that would come out like a present."

When she finished, a little girl jumped up, walked out into the aisle, turned around to the entire congregation, and said in a loud and clear voice, "What she means is," and then the girl stopped to catch her breath. "What she means is that our words should be like a little silver box with a bow on top."

Praise is not only welcomed by children. It goes a long way in the business world as well.

PEOPLE WORK FOR MONEY BUT GO THE EXTRA MILE FOR RECOGNITION, PRAISE, AND REWARDS

□

Chapter—10

Handling Mistakes, Complaints, and Criticism

Shortly after the close of World War I, I learned an invaluable lesson one night in London. 1 was attending a banquet given in honor of Sir Ross Smith. During the dinner, the man sitting next to me told a humorous story which hinged on the quotation, "There's a divinity that shapes our ends, rough-hew them how we will."

The raconteur mentioned that the quotation was from the Bible. He was wrong. I knew that. I knew it positively. There couldn't be the slightest doubt about it. And so, to get a feeling of importance and display my superiority, I appointed myself as an unsolicited and unwelcome committee of one to correct him. He stuck to his guns.

"What?" he thundered at me. "From Shakespeare? Impossible! Absurd!" That quotation was from the Bible, and he knew it with not one scintilla of doubt.

The storyteller was sitting on my right and Frank Gammond, an old friend of mine, was seated at my left. Frank had devoted years to the study of Shakespeare. So the storyteller and I agreed to submit the question to him. Frank listened, kicked me under the table, and then he said, "Dale, you are wrong. The gentleman is right. It is from the Bible."

I couldn't wait to get Frank alone. On our way home that night, 1 said to him, "Frank, you knew that quotation was from Shakespeare." "Yes, of course," he replied. "Hamlet, act five, scene two. But Dale, we were guests at a festive occasion. Why prove to a man he is wrong? Is that going to make him like you? Why not let him save his face? He didn't ask for your opinion. He didn't want it. Why argue with him?"

—DALE CARNEGIE

Barend Hendrik Strydom was a vicious, cold-blooded killer. Strydom, a white South African, was angry about the progress blacks were finally making in that land of racial apartheid. So one day in 1988 he decided to do something about it. He sprayed a crowd of black protesters with machine-gun fire, hitting nine men and women, leaving eight of them dead.

He was tried, convicted, and sent off to death row. But even then he didn't seem to think he had done anything to be criticized about. "To have remorse, one must have done something wrong," he said. "I have done nothing wrong."

When a legal technicality got Strydom's sentence changed from the death penalty to life in jail, he still didn't seem to understand the public outcry that his crime had caused. "I'll kill again," he said. "I have done nothing wrong."

If such a brutal killer doesn't blame himself for his horrific crime, what about the people most of us come into contact with every day? Do you think they're eager to admit mistakes or be criticized?

There are two fundamental facts about mistakes. Number one, we all make 'em. Number two, we're more than happy to point them out in others, but boy, how we hate it when someone points out one of ours!

Noel Coward was as thin-skinned about criticism as anyone, but at least he had a sense of humor. "I love criticism just so long as it's unqualified praise," the English playwright said.

No one—absolutely no one—likes to be on the receiving end of a complaint, a criticism, or a rotten review. We allbristle when the finger of responsibility is pointed at us. This is easy enough to understand. Nothing stings the ego like being told we've made a bad decision or supervised a failed project or performed below expectations. It's even more difficult when the criticism turns out to be correct.

But mistakes get made. Arguments arise. Complaints, both legitimate and exaggerated, get lodged day after day. Customers are unhappy. Nobody is on target all the time. So how do you handle the knowledge that nobody's perfect but criticism is hard to swallow? With a little practice and the help of a few time-tested human-relations techniques. Let's not deny the obvious. It's not always easy keeping both balls in the air. But it's not impossible either. After a while this particular juggling act can be mastered by almost anyone.

The first step is to create an environment where people are open to receiving advice or constructive criticism. Spread the word again and again that mistakes are a natural part of life.

One sure way to get this message across is to admit your own mistakes. "Setting the example is very important. You can't expect from others what you're not willing to expect from yourself." So says Fred Sievert of New York Life Insurance Company. Shortly after he arrived at the company, Sievert had an opportunity to put his ego where his mouth was.

Sievert explains, "I did something here that kind of astounded people. I was off in France at an executive management school, and we had some critical data that had to be submitted. It was our five-year plan, and there was a misunderstanding because it was my first time through this. Just before I left, we submitted the numbers. I was gone for two weeks. Of course, I was in touch via voice mail and fax. But we submitted the numbers, and there was a major crisis that occurred here. The problem was that I misunderstood the timing of this submission. I thought the initial submission was meant to be our first run of the numbers. I thought we then had plenty of time to analyze and talk about management actions that could be taken to improve the numbers. As it turns out, I didn't understand the process, and the first set of numbers that were given to the executive management committee and the chairman were viewed as our version of the plan. I didn't know that.

"Well, it created a tremendous problem because the numbers weren't good. There were inconsistencies. There were management actions we hadn't reflected, and I was off in France sending these voice mails back and forth, not really understanding what had happened but knowing there was a crisis. I volunteered to come back, but my boss said, 'No, we got it handled.'

"When I got back I realized what had happened. After talking to various people —I know these people were shocked —I said at a meeting, 'This is my fault. It's a communication issue. It wasn't a matter of not understanding the numbers. It was a matter of communication, and it was entirely my fault.'

"While I was gone, people were pointing the finger at each other. My staff was saying, 'Why didn't you guys tell us this was our last shot at this?' And the other people were saying, 'You should have understood this was the last shot.' Okay, everybody's pointing the finger, and I came in and stood up and said, 'This is entirely my fault. I take full responsibility for it. It's a communication problem. It won't happen again.' And you know that statement put an end to all the finger pointing. Several people in the room said, 'No, no, no, it wasn't your fault. You know it was a combination of people.'"

Readily admitting fault —it's one of the best ways anyone has ever invented for shifting momentum when blame is being distributed. Be the first to admit mistakes. Everyone else will rush to reassure you, 'No, it's not so bad; no, it doesn't really matter; no, they probably were to blame; no, it all turned out fine in the end.'

Take the opposite tack —blame other people for something—and just as quickly they'll start to contradict you, and they'll defend the correctness of their actions. Funny, isn't it, how human psychology works?

This is true for all relationships—inside a company, a family, or a group of friends. And it's true in customer or vendor relationships as well.

When a customer is unhappy about a product or the service that's been provided, a quick and forceful admission of error can often work wonders. That's what John Imlay discovered when he inadvertently offended an important customer. "Back in 1987," recalls Imlay, chairman of Dun & Bradstreet Software, "I had to give a speech on the west coast of the United States to a group of chief information officers, I guess about a thousand of them. It was out at the Laguna Beach Hotel. To open it, I was talking about what's in and what out. 'Noriega's out, democracy's in.' Things like that. And the last one was, 'Teenage Mutant Ninja Turtles are in, Ken and Barbie are out.' Everybody laughed except one fellow, one of my key customers. He was the head of Mattel.

"So before I returned to the office, I received a letter. The letter said, 'I enjoyed your speech, but you made one statement that I want you to retract forever.' He went on in a blistering way, finally summing up by saying the sales of Barbie were more than the revenues of all my companies combined. So I wrote him a letter apologizing, and I wrote Barbie a letter. He didn't think that was funny, either."

Did Imlay give up there? Absolutely not. "For years," he said, "I took his letter and put it into a slot, and every speech I gave I reminded the audience how you have to be sensitive to the customer's issues, and customers absolutely love the slot. I showed the letter, and how I had gotten it.

"One day I spoke at the Waldorf-Astoria in New York, and the president of Mattel was there. I gave this speech not knowing he was in the audience. As I spoke, someone passed me a note saying that the president of Mattel was there. I had him stand up, and he came up and shook my hand. Then he dropped me a note afterward saying all is forgiven, and he's been a happy customer ever since." The lesson here: Admit your mistakes before anyone else has a chance to point them out. Laugh about them if you can. Never seek to minimize the impact they've had. "A leader has to be responsible and accountable for his or her own mistakes," says Fred Sievert. "The worst thing you can do is to begin to point your finger at everybody else. You've got to take responsibility." Or as Andres Navarro says, "If an organization is able to admit mistakes, it's encouraging creativity and encouraging people to take risks."

The second step for handling mistakes or problems: Think twice before you criticize or assign blame. If the person who made the mistake already knows how it happened, why it happened, and what needs to be done so it won't happen again, then nothing at all needs to be said. There's no point in making people feel worse than they already do.

Motivated employees want to perform well. G. Curt Jones, senior quality executive at the Federal Quality Institute, says, "People don't come to work to mess up. They want to feel needed. They want to be committed." Business leaders who understand that understand how destructive most criticism is.

The point is avoiding the blame game, and Ray Stata, the chairman of Analog Devices, Inc., knows all about it.

"The instinctive question when something goes wrong is, 'Who's to blame?'" Stata observes. "It's the way the human mind is wired. You want to find somebody to blame and talk about their mistakes."

Stata is trying to rid Analog Devices of all unnecessary blame. "One of the things that I'm cutting out is preaching in the organization," he said. "We all tend to do it. You know, commiserate, blame, when things aren't going right. Now, I think one of the little tricks is for me to set the example of converting complaints into requests and suggestions."

You have to ask yourself, What am I trying to accomplish here? Says Stata: "At the end of the day, what you want to do is create effective action that makes the place better. And talking about who was wrong or what's to blame is not it." The real goal is to improve the situation.

Jack Gallagher had a major problem on his hands. Gallagher is the president of North Shore University Hospital, a 755-bed institution affiliated with Cornell University Medical College. As North Shore grew over the years, the hospital was stuck with the same kitchen that had been adequate in the days of 169 beds.

When the time finally came to build a new kitchen, Gallagher asked an associate to oversee the job. He gave the man two pieces of advice: hire a parking consultant and hire a dietary consultant.

"I couldn't follow the project every day," Gallagher recalls. "And for some reason, he didn't use the parking consultant. He didn't use the dietary consultant. So we got trapped between the opening of the new kitchen and the closing of the old."

By the time Gallagher discovered this, construction was already under way and millions had already been spent. It was much too late to change the plans. But no one was happy with the results. The new kitchen was too small, the quality of the food was slipping, and the hospital's reputation was suffering as a result.

Gallagher could have fired the associate. He could have criticized the man in public. But what good would that have done? How would a public scolding have improved the lamb chops or the baked chicken? Would it have made the string beans stay hot?

"You don't want to point a finger and assign blame," Gallagher says. "What we had to do was fix the system. We had to make it better. We had to step back and say, 'How can we improve the situation?' Blame wouldn't have gotten us any closer to that."

Criticism or blame spreading almost always causes people to duck and hide. People who have been on the receiving end of harsh criticism are far less likely to take risks, to be creative, to go out on a limb of any kind. Instantly the organization has lost an important part of that employee's potential.

This concept has found its way into the whole employee-review process at Mary Kay Corporation. The goal is improvement, not judgment. "We don't call that a performance appraisal, we call it performance development," said Mary Kay Vice Chairman Richard Bartlett. Why's that? "I don't want to sit there and be judgmental," Bartlett says. "I want to know how I can help you be better. The big thing is we're sitting down and discussing your career at Mary Kay. How do you need to develop to be whatever it is you want to be in the future? From your viewpoint." Now that's the kind of corporate attitude that invites and encourages employee innovation.

"The people who accept criticism the best are the people who are genuinely interested in self-improvement," according to David Luther, the Corning quality chief. "Sometimes the easiest people to correct are those who are at the top of the league. They're the people who are going for the extra five percent and welcome constructive criticism. One of the advantages of the Japanese is their notion of treasuring errors. They consider the discovery of a mistake or error as a treasure because it's a key toward further improvement."

We all agree: almost no one likes to receive it, and far too many people like to give it. Blaming someone rarely improves the situation.

There are exceptions, of course. Sometimes people do need to be criticized constructively. If the need is urgent enough, if the danger is severe enough, and if the mistake is made often enough, then something needs to be said. If after thoughtful consideration, you do decide you have to discuss a situation, criticize respectfully.

That's step number three. Walk softly and leave the big stick at home. Restrain yourself, follow a few basic techniques, and you'll ensure that your words are met by open ears. Hi Create a receptive environment for what you have to say. While people don't ever like to hear negative things about themselves, they'll be more receptive if you focus on the things they do right as well as the things they do wrong.

"The process of criticism should begin with praise and honest appreciation," Dale Carnegie said. Mary Poppins had much the same thing in mind when she sang, "A spoonful of sugar helps the medicine go down."

Andres Navarro at SONDA, S.A., has found a way to institutionalize a kinder, gentler approach to criticism. In his company there is now a three-for-one rule. Navarro explains, "We try to criticize as little as we can. We have a rule. If you get into this company and you find someone whom you don't like and you think doesn't do his work the way he should, don't say anything. Write it down on a piece of paper. Once you discover three good things about the person whom you're talking about—or about a policy or a rule or a habit that we have —then you have the right to criticize one." That's a great technique.

Another one is using encouragement. Make the faults seem easy to correct. This is the same principle that is practiced by New York Life's Fred Sievert. He calls it his "sandwich technique" for giving criticism. "I start by talking about the positive things that the employee has accomplished," Sievert says. "Then in the middle we talk about the areas for development and improvement. Finally we close with a discussion of how valuable the person is to New York Life. It always works. I had a boss once who did that with me, and I used to walk out of the room scratching my head, saying, 'Gee, I really feel good about getting reprimanded.'"

Equally important is knowing what to avoid. Never argue, demean, or shout at someone. If you're arguing with someone, you've already lost. You've lost control of yourself, you've lost your perspective, and most significantly, you've lost sight of your goal: to communicate, to persuade, to motivate. As Dale Carnegie said, "There is only one way under high heaven to get the best of an argument— and that is to avoid it. Avoid it as you would avoid rattlesnakes and earthquakes. Nine times out of ten, an argument ends with each of the contestants being more firmly convinced than ever that he is absolutely right."

Let the person save face at all costs. This may mean hanging back in a discussion, calling attention to the person's mistakes indirectly, or asking questions instead of giving orders. Or it may mean saving some criticism for another day. However you choose to do it, the goal is the same: be gentle, underplay, don't attack. Even if someone doesn't agree entirely with your point of view, with enough finesse you may still get that person to see some merit in your position. But if you come on too strong, if you use words like right and wrong, smart and stupid, you'll never persuade anyone of anything.

"We do get complaints," Wolfgang Schmitt of Rubbermaid says. "About half of those complaints come about as the result of a consumer's buying a product, thinking it's ours, but it's a competitor's product. So the consumer writes to us. Our policy is simply to write a personal letter and say, 'We can understand how You made the mistake because we have these competitors who copy our products. You made an honest mistake, but we would like for you to see directly the difference in value. So try one of ours for free.'

"We send them our replacement product for whatever it is they complained about. And we think that's a wonderful way to communicate very credibly the story of Rubbermaid value."

Gentle persuasion always works better than screaming and finger pointing. When you need to remind yourself of this, recall the old Aesop fable about the contest between the wind and the sun. The wind and the sun argued one day over which was stronger. The wind proposed a contest and, seeing an old man walking down the street, set the terms of the bet: whoever could get the man to remove his coat first would win. The sun agreed and the wind went first. The wind blew, harder and harder, until the gusts 1 almost reached tornado force. But the harder the wind blew, the tighter the man clutched his coat.

When the wind gave up, the sun had its chance. The sun shone on the man gently, becoming warmer and warmer until the man, wiping his brow, took off his coat. The sun told the wind its secret: gentleness and friendliness are stronger than force and fury. The same rule applies to customers, to employees, to coworkers, to friends.

Dale Carnegie had a student in one of his classes who was a tax consultant. The student, Frederick Parsons, had a disagreement with an IRS agent about how to classify a nine-thousand-dollar debt. Parsons was arguing that the money was a bad debt that had not been paid and therefore wasn't taxable income. The agent was equally adamant that it was taxable.

Parsons was getting nowhere. So he decided to try a different approach: "I decided to avoid the argument, change the subject, and give him appreciation. I said, 'I suppose this is a very petty matter in comparison with the really important and difficult decisions you're required to make. I've made a study of taxation myself, but I've had to get my knowledge from books. You are getting yours from the firing line of experience. I sometimes wish I had a job like yours. It would teach me a lot' I meant every word."

The result? "The inspector straightened up in his chair, leaned back, and talked for a long time about his work, telling me of the clever frauds he had uncovered. His tone gradually became friendly, and soon he was telling me about his children. As he left, he advised me that he would consider my problem further and give me his decision in a few days. He called at my office three days later and informed me that he had decided to leave the tax return exactly as it had been filed."

What changed the tax inspector's mind? "The tax inspector was demonstrating one of the most common of human frailties," Carnegie wrote. "He wanted a feeling of importance. As long as Mr. Parsons argued with him, he got his feeling of importance by loudly asserting his authority. But as soon as his importance was admitted and the argument stopped and he was permitted to expand his ego, he became a sympathetic and kindly human being "

BE QUICK TO ADMIT MISTAKES AND SLOW TO CRITICIZE. ABOVE ALL, BE CONSTRUCTIVE.

□

Chapter—11
Setting Goals

At age twenty-three I was one of the unhappiest young men in New York. I was selling motor trucks for a living. I didn't know what made a motor truck run. That wasn't all: I didn't want to know. I despised my job. I despised living in a cheap furnished room on West Fifty-sixth Street—a room infested with cockroaches. I still remember that I had a bunch of neckties hanging on the walls, and when I reached out every morning to get a fresh necktie, the cockroaches scattered in all directions. I despised having to eat in cheap, dirty restaurants that were also probably infested with cockroaches.

I came home to my lonely room each night with a sick headache—a headache bred and fed by disappointment, worry, bitterness, and rebellion. I was rebelling because the dreams I had nourished back in my college days had turned into nightmares. Was this life? Was this the vital adventure to which I had looked forward so eagerly? Was this all life would ever mean to me—working at a job I despised and with no hope for the future? I longed for leisure to read. I longed to write the books I had dreamed of writing back in my college days.

I knew I had everything to gain and nothing to lose by giving up the job I despised. I wasn't interested in making a lot of money, but I was interested in making a lot of living. In short, I had come to the Rubicon - to that moment of decision which faces most young people when they set out in life. So I made my decision, and that decision completely altered my future. It has made the rest of my life happy and rewarding beyond my most My decision was this: 1 would give up the work I loathed, and since I had spent four years studying in the State Teachers College at Warrensburg, Missouri, preparing to teach, I would make my living teaching adult classes in night schools. Then I would have my days free to read books, prepare lectures, write novels and short stories. I wanted "to live to write and write to live."

—DALE CARNEGIE

Dale Carnegie never wrote the great American novel, but his remarkable success as a teacher, a businessman, and a writer of human-relations books has made him an inspiration to people around the world. He achieved all that by setting goals for himself, adjusting those goals as circumstances required, and trying never to lose sight of where he was headed next.

Mary Lou Retton was just a high-school sophomore from West Virginia, a state that had never once produced a world-class gymnast.

"I was a nobody," she says, "and I was number one in the state." She was a tiny fourteen-year-old, performing at a competition in Reno, Nevada. That's the day the great BelaKarolyi, the Romanian gymnastics coach who had guided Nadia Comaneci to Olympic gold, walked up behind Mary Lou.

"He was the king of gymnastics," Retton recalls. "He came up to me. He tapped me on the shoulder. He's a big man—six-three or six-four. He came up to me and said, 'Mary Lou/ in that deep Romanian accent. 'You come to me, and I will make you Olympic champion."

The first thought that went racing through Retton's mind was, "Yeah, right. No way."

But of all the gymnasts in that Nevada arena, BelaKarolyi

had noticed her. "So we sat down, and we talked," Retton remembers. "He talked with my parents and said, 'Listen, there's no guarantee that Mary Lou will even make the Olympic team, but I think she's got the material that it takes.'"

What a goal that was! Since early childhood she had harbored dreams about one day performing in the Olympics. But hearing the words come out of the great man's mouth —as far as Retton was concerned, that set the goal in stone.

"It was a very big risk for me," she says. "I was going to be moving away from my family and my friends, living with a family I had never met before, training with girls I didn't know. It pumped me up so much. I was scared. I didn't know what to expect. But I was excited too. This man wanted to train me. Little me, from Fairmont, West Virginia. I had been picked out."

And she wasn't about to let Karolyi down. It was two and a half years later that Mary Lou Retton, after a pair of perfect tens, won the Olympic gold medal in gymnastics for America —and with it a place in the hearts of people everywhere.

Goals give us something to shoot for. They keep our efforts focused. They allow us to measure our success.

So set goals—goals that are challenging but also realistic, goals that are clear and measurable, goals for the short term and goals for the long term.

When you reach one goal, take a second to pat yourself on the back. Then move on to the next goal, emboldened, strengthened, energized by what you've already achieved.

Eugene Lang, a New York City philanthropist, was making a graduation speech to a sixth-grade class at PS 121. This class had a group of children with absolutely no hope of ever going to college. In fact, there was very little hope that most of these children would even graduate from high school. But at the end of the graduation speech, Lang made a stunning offer. "For any of you who graduate from high school, I will ensure that funds are available for you to go to college," he said. Of the forty-eight students in that sixth-grade class that day, forty-four graduated from high school and forty-two went to college. To put that into perspective, remember that forty percent of inner-city students never graduate from high school, let alone go to college.

That monetary offer alone wasn't enough to ensure such great success. Lang also made sure that the students got the support they needed along the way. They were monitored and counseled through their last six years of school. But that one challenging goal, clearly articulated and within the students' reach, gave them an opportunity to visualize a future they never thought was possible. And by visualizing it for themselves, they were able to make their dreams reality.

In the words of Harvey Mackay, the best-selling business author, "A goal is a dream with a deadline."

Howard Marguleas is the chairman of a produce company called Sun World, and he's one of California's new breed of growers. He got to be that way by setting and meeting goal after goal. For years Marguleas had watched as the agriculture business went up and down—fat times, lean times, as impossible to predict as they were to control. At least that's how everyone said the fruit-and-vegetable business worked.

But Marguleas had a goal: to develop new and unique kinds of produce that could withstand the shifts in the tides of consumer buying. "This business is really no different from real estate," Marguleas reasoned. "When the market's down, unless you have something very highly, uniquely different, you're in serious trouble. Same thing in agriculture. If you're just another producer of lettuce, carrots, or oranges, and you have nothing different from anyone else, you do well only if there's a short supply. If there's a large supply, you won't do well. And that's what we've tried to adjust to, to find the windows of opportunity that come with being different, a niche in the marketplace."

That's where the idea of a better pepper came from. Yes, a better pepper. If he could develop a pepper that was tastier than the peppers that other people grew, Marguleas assured himself, wouldn't the grocers of America want to stock it in good times and in bad?

So he did it, giving birth to the Le Rouge Royal pepper. "It's an elongated, three-lobe pepper," Marguleas says. "We were told, you know, 'You have to have a bell pepper, a square-shaped pepper, to sell.' But once we tasted this pepper —the color, the flavor, everything about it—we knew we had something. We knew that if we promoted it properly and advertised and merchandised it and put a name on it, we could get people to eat it. And once they ate it, they were going to continue to buy it."

What all this taught Marguleas is, "Never cease to pursue the opportunity to seek something different. Don't be satisfied with what you're doing. Always try to seek a way and a method to improve upon what you're doing, even if it's considered contrary to the traditions of an industry."

Those who fail to establish independent goals for themselves become, in Marguleas's word, the "me-toos" of the world. The me-toos, the people who follow but don't lead, do fine when times are good. But when times get tough, they inevitably get left behind.

Marguleas had his finger on something there. People who set goals—challenging goals, but goals that are also achievable—are the ones with solid grips on their futures, the ones who end up accomplishing extraordinary things. Reebok International, Ltd., the athletic-shoe company, set a major corporate goal for itself: get Shaquille O'Neal. The Orlando Magic star wasn't going to come easy. Lots of major companies were eager to hire him as their spokesman. "It was a question of convincing him that we had the best commitment to him, that we were willing to do something to create for him a program that the next guy couldn't do," says Paul Fireman, Reebok's chairman.

The whole company geared up. "We created an ad campaign before he was here. We created it for him exclusively. We spent money to create it, and we really put our effort in. We were just absolutely committed to getting him. We took a gamble. We took a risk. We spent the money, the time, and the commitment." Sometimes that's what setting goals is all about.

"It would have been a major confrontation emotionally if we had lost," Fireman said. "If we didn't go so far to get him here, we wouldn't have had the loss emotionally. But we wouldn't have had the player, either."

Goals aren't important only for companies. They're the building blocks that successful careers are made of.

Jack Gallagher worked in the family tire business, where he had held just about every job—accounting, bookkeeping, manufacturing, and sales. All that experience in the tire business taught him one thing for sure: he didn't want to work in the tire business.

One day Gallagher ran into a high-school friend who was working as an assistant administrator at a local hospital. "That's what I'd like to do," Gallagher told himself. "I'd love to help people. I'd love to have a big business, and I'd love to lead a group for the right things." There were several giant hurdles between Jack Gallagher and a hospital administrator's job —a graduate degree in hospital administration, for one thing, and a job at a hospital, for another. But Gallagher had his goal, and he got started jumping the hurdles right away.

He talked his way into Yale. He won a stipend from the Kellogg Foundation. He got a loan from a local bank. He worked nights in the business office of North Shore University Hospital. And after he got the graduate degree, he applied for an administrative residency at North Shore.

"I interviewed with Jack Hausman, the chairman of the hospital's board," Gallagher recalls. "I must have spent three minutes with him, and I sold him in three minutes. He asked me a funny question. He knew I was married and had three kids. He said, 'How are you going to afford it?' They paid thirty-nine hundred for a resident then." Gallagher recalls how he responded: "Look, Mr. Hausman, I thought it out a long time before I came to see you here. I had to have everything set so I could live during this residency and move into an administrative role after that."

He had a goal. He planned every detail. He worked tirelessly toward them. He's North Shore's CEO today.

Singer-songwriter Nail Sedaka, whose pop-music career has spanned more than three decades, learned to set goals when he was just a kid. Sedaka grew up in a rough part of Brooklyn, and he was never one of the tough guys. His earliest goal was a perfectly understandable one: to be liked and thereby stay alive through high school.

"I wasn't a fighter," Sedaka explained recently. "So I had to be liked. I always wanted to be liked. You know how it is. You're always afraid of getting into a fight." Anyway, young Neil came up with what turned out to be an ingenious method of achieving his personal goal—music.

"There was a sweetshop near Lincoln High School, and there was a jukebox in the back," he recalled. "All the tough kids, the leather-set kids, would hang out there, and they would listen to Elvis and Fats Domino. This was the beginning of rock and roll. So I wrote a rock-and-roll song, and I sang it, and then I was like a hero with those leather-set kids. They even let me into their part of the sweetshop."

The point here isn't whether Sedaka should have cared about acceptance from the tough kids. These things can seem awfully important in the high-school years. But he knew instinctively how to reach these other people —and how to achieve what was important to him at the time. For Sedaka, that high-school goal turned into a lifelong career, and this early success gave him the confidence to shoot for the stars in the future.

Much the same process unfolded in the early life of

Arthur Ashe, the late tennis champion. Almost singlehandedly, Ashe broke down the color barrier in professional tennis, a game that until he came along had been almost exclusively white. In his later years, Ashe fought a valiant battle against the AIDS virus, raising consciousness about the disease on ghetto street corners and in townhouse drawing rooms.

His was a life of setting and reaching goals. For Ashe it started when he was a youngster on a tennis court. That's where he learned about achievement, one goal at a time.

"Breaking through that barrier, where you have set a goal and you achieve that goal, it sort of codifies whatever budding self-confidence you might have had," Ashe said in an interview for this book just before his death.

That's how Ashe operated until the day he died. He'd set a goal and when he'd met that goal, he'd set another one. Why? "The self-confidence itself, I think, transforms the individual," he explained. "It also spills over into other areas of life. Not only do you feel confident in whatever you are expert at, but you probably feel generally self-confident that you can do some other things as well, applying the same principles maybe to another task or to another set of goals."

The goals must be realistic, and they must be attainable. Don't make the mistake of thinking you should, or can, accomplish everything today. Maybe you can't reach the moon this year, so plan a shorter trip. Set an interim goal.

Following that incremental approach, Ashe put himself on the big-time tennis map. "My early coaches," explained Ashe, "set out definite goals which I bought into. The goals were not necessarily winning tennis tournaments. The goals were just things that we saw as difficult, that would require some hard work and some planning. And there was sort of an implied reward out there if I achieved those goals. Again, the goal wasn't necessarily winning this tournament or that tournament. And so incrementally, before I knew it, after I attained these mini goals along the way, all of a sudden, 'Hey, I'm close to the big prize here.'"

That's how Ashe always approached tough tennis matches. "In a tournament, you'd want to get to the quarterfinals. Or in a match, you would want to not miss acertain number of backhand passing shots. Or maybe you'd want to improve your stamina to a point where you're not going to get tired when the weather is too hot. Those are the sorts of goals that help take your general focus off that long-range, elusive goal— the goal of being number one or winning the whole tournament."

Most big challenges are best faced with a series of interim goals. That's a far more encouraging process —far more motivating too.

Dr. James D. Watson, the director of the Cold Spring Harbor Laboratory, has been locked in a lifelong struggle to find the cure for cancer. Is that his only goal? Of course not. That would be too discouraging for anyone to bear. Watson has laid out a series of incremental goals for himself and his laboratory colleagues, goals they are meeting every year on the road to the ultimate cure.

"There are so many different cancers," explains Watson, who won a Nobel prize for discovering the structure of DNA. "We're going to cure some of them. Hopefully, we'll cure more of them.

"But you've got to pick interim goals," he says. "The goal is not to kill colon cancer tomorrow. It's to understand the disease. And there are many different steps. No one wants to be led into defeat. You get your happiness one small goal at a time."

That's the way it works. Set little goals. Meet them. Set new, slightly larger goals. Meet them. Succeed.

Long before Lou Holtz became Notre Dame's head football coach, he wanted nothing more than to play the game himself. But when he went out for his high-school team, he weighed just 115 pounds.

Holtz knew this was far too small. Still, he desperately wanted to play, so he came up with a plan. He memorized all eleven positions on the team. That way, if any player got hurt, he was immediately prepared to rush onto the field. It gave him eleven chances instead of one. "It's the same way in business today," says writer Harvey Mackay. "If you're working out here in the office, volunteer to learn the phone system. Volunteer to know what's going on in computers. If you're in sales, you want to know about computers." That way, when opportunities appear, you'll have a much greater chance of seizing them. Set goals that make you more valuable to your team—as Lou Holtz did—or to your company.

The idea is to set goals and then strive to meet them. Sometimes you'll succeed on schedule, sometimes things will take longer to achieve than you thought, and sometimes you won't attain what you thought you would. Some things just aren't meant to be. The point is to keep planning and plugging away. You'll get there, just watch.

As Scalamandre Silks' Adriana Bitter says: "Maybe we set our goals too high sometimes and we don't always reach the top end, but we certainly can start climbing that ladder."

Without specific goals it's far too easy just to drift, never really taking charge of your life. Time gets wasted because nothing has a sense of urgency. There's no deadline. Nothing has to be done today. It's possible to put off anything indefinitely. Goals are what can give us direction and keep us focused.

David Luther of Corning is acutely aware of this modern propensity toward aimlessness. He worries about how it might affect his own children at home. So he's constantly talking to them about goals.

"Sometimes," he reminds them, "we get caught up in things." Easy to say, of course, but how to avoid this pitfall? "The point," according to Luther, "is to know yourself. Think what it is that you know and want to do. Forget the money, for a moment anyway. When you get to be the age of your parents, what is it you want to be able to point to that met your expectation, that made a difference?"

How are intelligent goals created? Mostly they just take a little thought, but there are some useful techniques for getting the mind focused on the task. You might try asking yourself the same questions Luther urges his children toask. "Stand back and say, 'What is it I really want to be? What kind of life do I really want to lead? Am I heading in the right direction now?'" That advice makes sense no matter how far along you are in your career.

Once you establish what your goals are, prioritize them. Not everything can be done at once, so you've got to ask yourself, Which comes first? What goal is most important to me now? Then try organizing your time and energy to reflect those priorities. This, often, is the most challenging part.

To prioritize his goals, Ted Owen, publisher of the San Diego Business Journal, follows the advice he got from a psychologist friend. "He told me to take a piece of paper and draw a line down the center. On the left, put any number you want. I put ten. Put the top ten things that you want to accomplish in your life before you retire at whatever age that is, one hundred or sixty or fifty.

"Put down those ten things. So you want to have a good retirement program. You want to have a nice home. You want to have a happy marriage. You want to have good health. Whatever those ten are. Then over here on the other side, you take those ten and prioritize them. One of those ten becomes number one, and so on."

Simplistic? Maybe. But helpful too. Through this process, Owen discovered some things about himself he never knew. "I found out that a job, a well-paying, steady job, a job that makes me feel good, was about number seven." Once you identify your own number one, two, three, and seven, creating well-crafted goals becomes a whole lot easier.

It's fine if, over the years, those goals develop and change. "Before I was married, I would come in on the weekends just to read the newspaper here," says Dr. Ronald Evans, a research professor at the Salk Institute for Biological Studies. "I had nothing else to do. I loved being in labs. It was sort of a home away from home. Research is addicting," he observes. "It's incredibly challenging and pushes your intellectual limits. You make discoveries, and there's nothing like it." But life changes, pressures change, and goals should be evaluated too. "With a family now," Evans goes on, "it's been very difficult to change my habits, but I have. You just have to say you can't do everything."

Corporations need goals as much as individuals do, and the same basic rules apply when companies begin defining theirs: make them clear, keep them basic, and don't set too many at once.

The huge Motorola corporation was run in one recent year with just three specific goals, expressed in precise, mathematical terms: to "continue 10-X improvement" every two years, to "get the voice of" the customer, to "cut business-process cycle time by factor 10" in five years.

Don't worry about what this language means. It may or may not apply at your company. What's important here is that the company has its goals. These goals are clearly understood within the company. The goals are challenging but attainable. Progress is easily measurable. And if these goals are achieved, the company will have done extraordinarily well.

Those three specific goals provide enough vision to run an entire company. Imagine what three equally clear, equally realistic goals can do for one person's life.

SET GOALS THAT ARE CLEAR, CHALLENGING, AND OBTAINABLE.

□

Chapter—12

Focus and Discipline

Back in 1933, David Burpee, famous seed man of Philadelphia, got the idea that the plain, everyday stepchild of flowers could be made very beautiful and attractive. That stepchild was the marigold, a forlorn but little waif with a most unfortunate trait: an unpleasant odor.

So David Burpee set out to develop a marigold that would titillate instead of shock the nostrils. He knew there was just one way to do this, and that was to find what botanists call a mutation, an individual flower, which by accident, doesn't have this unpleasant odor. So he sent all over the world for marigold seed and got 640 separate cultures. He planted them and when they grew and blossomed, he pushed his nose against them and sniffed. Every single one had a bad odor. Pretty discouraging, but he kept searching, and finally a missionary in far-off Tibet sent him some seed of a marigold that was odorless but had a scrawny flower.

David Burpee crossed this with one of his large varieties and planted thirty-five acres. When they were up and going strong, he called his foreman and gave an order that made the foreman think that David Burpee had gone crazy. He told his foreman to get down on his hands and knees and smell every plant in the thirty-five acres. If just one odorless plant with large flowers could be found, that would be all that was needed. "It would take me thirty-five years to smell them all," said the foreman. So the employment agencies in that section were called up to be given an order like they had never before received, an order for two hundred flower smellers.

These flower smellers came from everywhere and started to work. No one ever saw a crazier sight, but Dave Burpee knew what he was doing. At last, one day, one of the flower smellers came loping across the field to the foreman.

"I've got it," he shouted. The foreman followed him to the place where the smeller had stuck down a peg. Sure enough, there wasn't a hint of an unpleasant odor.

—DALE CARNEGIE

Margaret Thatcher led Britain through some of the most difficult years in the empire's history—a time that included the Falklands War, a worldwide recession, and enough social upheaval to fill a century or two. Those years wrecked any number of promising political careers, and as the prime minister of Britain (not to mention the first woman ever to hold that job), Thatcher took more than her share of the heat. Yet there was one thing people on all sides of British politics had to admit: the Iron Lady never melted once. How did she manage such strength under pressure?

"If you lead a country like Britain," Thatcher explained shortly after stepping down, "a strong country, a country that has taken a lead in world affairs in good times and in bad, a country that is always reliable, then you have to have a touch of iron about you."

It's really not so complicated, the former prime minister said. Stay focused. Be self-disciplined. Want desperately to succeed. "I do not know anyone who has got to the top without hard work," she went on. "That is the recipe. It will not always get you to the top, but it should get you pretty near."

Maggie Thatcher understood. Have a goal clearly in mind, something you really want; believe in yourself and be persistent; and don't allow yourself to be distracted. In business, in family life, in sports, in politics, follow these simple rules, and your chances of succeeding are astronomically high Ivan Stewart was a man with a goal. He had a life-long dream of competing in long-distance off-road auto racing— races of three hundred, five hundred, one thousand miles across rugged terrain, involving hours and hours of intense concentration and intense backaches. But Stewart was a general superintendent in the construction business with a wife, a mortgage, and three growing kids. He had responsibilities. He had commitments. The odds were way against his reaching his goal, but he also had a plan and lots of energy to pursue it.

"I wanted to be involved in racing, so I worked on the race cars after work and on Saturday and Sunday. Then I got a chance to ride, just to be involved, never thinking at the time—not at all —that it would ever get professional," Stewart says.

One day his opportunity arrived. A driver Stewart had been working with broke his leg just before a race. The car was ready and entered. He had no choice but to let Stewart drive.

So with his friend Earl Stahl sitting in the passenger seat, Stewart set out in the race. Everything went to hell. They ran into an embankment. The car flipped over. They got stuck in the mud. The other cars were whizzing by. His one chance of proving himself looked irretrievably lost.

"By now we're the last car," he says, recalling that very first race. "Everybody's gone. They start one car every thirty seconds, and there were probably sixty cars, seventy cars in that race. Everybody's gone. Here's Earl and I, now we're last. We didn't go another ten miles, fifteen miles, twenty miles, whatever it was, when the throttle —this is a Volkswagen-powered car—the cable that goes from your foot back to the carburetor broke. So now I can't even drive. I said, 'Earl, get a crescent wrench.' Earl gets the crescent wrench out of the tool box, and I pull out the wire that's broken, and it's just long enough to pull around the crescent wrench so I can wrap it around the crescent. We do this pretty quick. Within five or ten minutes we've got a hand throttle going so I can push the throttle and I can push the clutch and I can drive one-handed. No power steering though. This is determination—and I want to drive.

"I said to Earl, 'I need you to shift it,' because it's a four-speed transmission. 'I'm going to give you an elbow every time I want to change.' So I'd push the throttle, and we were so messed up, I'd have the clutch in, the throttle on, and he'd be in the wrong gear. Anyway, we got going pretty good. I'd give the throttle and lay off the throttle. I'd push the clutch in and give him an elbow and he'd give me a higher gear. Pretty soon he realized what we wanted to do. We were messed up because once in a while he'd give me a low gear and I wanted a high gear and vice versa. But we got pretty good at it. Pretty soon we started catching—this is a three-hundred-mile race. We catch one, we catch another one. Teamwork. Yes, we got good at it. Pretty soon we were really driving. You know, we were driving, and to make a long story short, we won that race. Won that three-hundred-mile race." That kind of focus and self-discipline is what it takes to win the race in all parts of life.

Stewart went on to become the top off-road driver in America. He's won the prestigious Valvoline oil Iron Man trophy—the sport's He is mann and Super Bowl rolled into one—so many times that his fans now know him simply as Iron Man. And at forty-seven years old —ancient in this body-jarring sport— Stewart signed another three-year sponsorship deal with Toyota.

"They know I'm getting older, and there's a lot of young kids coming in." But that's just another challenge, not a reason to give up. Who knows? Iron Man will probably still be racing at sixty. It's that kind of focus—whatever the field of endeavor—that separates the achievers from the no achievers.

That's the single biggest secret to raising major money, says Thomas A. Saunders III at Saunders Karp & Company.

"When I was raising this big fund a few years ago for Morgan Stanley," Saunders recalls, "we had an assignment to go in and raise for our merchant banking business two hundred million dollars. We raised two-point-three billion. It was the second-largest amount of money that's ever been assembled for a pure equity fund. I think an awful lot of the success of that was just stick-to-itiveness, not being prepared to go in and be turned off. Not being prepared to accept no for an answer, a willingness to come back at it again. A willingness to keep pushing. A willingness to find out why someone said no—and maybe convince the person to say yes."

Fred Sievert is chief financial officer at New York Life Insurance Company. The person he learned his perseverance from was his father, whose name is also Fred. "The one love in his life was playing the trumpet," Sievert says of his father. "He played with some of the best big bands, including Harry James, Artie Shaw, and Jack Teagarden. He's a very exceptional trumpet player."

And even the father never stopped practicing the basics. "He would play scales," the son says. "Here's a guy who's already one of the best trumpet players in the country, and what's he doing? He's not playing some lengthy new tune that he wants to learn. He's playing the scales. Hour after hour, day after day. He would play these different scales. He would say to me that if he knew the scales and he could play them quickly, he could learn any song there was."

That same unshakable focus is what propelled two Southern governors, sixteen years apart, all the way to the White House. One was a soft-spoken peanut farmer from Georgia by the name of Jimmy Carter. The other came from a little dot on the map called Hope, Arkansas. His name is Bill Clinton.

When Carter started his 1976 campaign, few of the big-time national political pros gave him much of a chance. Hardly anyone outside Georgia had ever heard of him, he was facing a crowded field of higher-profile Democrats, and the campaign's first major hurdle was New Hampshire, about as far from home as this Georgian could get.

When Clinton ran in 1992, he was thought to face similarly long odds—and the reasons were mostly the same. He was a little better known than Carter had been, but not much so, and the sitting Republican president had just won a hugely popular war.

If you believed the early experts, neither one of these governors had much of a chance. By the end of the early primaries, these two sons of Dixie were supposed to be out of the running. That's not what happened, of course, and there are many reasons why. None of them was more important than the focus and the discipline of these two campaigns.

In the course of these grueling races, both men had many reasons to give up. For Carter, besides his utter obscurity, there was the threat of Ted Kennedy and the nagging perception that Kennedy, not Carter, was the choice of "real Democrats." For Clinton, there were the claims of Gennifer Flowers, the count-him-out editorials, the power of a sitting president, and a fellow named Perot.

Those odds didn't stop Carter in 1976. They didn't stop Clinton in 1992. And the biggest reason both times was that both men were focused. They knew exactly what they wanted to achieve. They were working toward a specific goal, a dream each man had held since childhood. As a result, they had superhuman motivation. They worked like crazy and kept their eyes on the ball, and they won the prize.

Persistence is the other part of the equation. To get what you want in life, you've got to believe in yourself and you've got to be willing to keep after it. Try again and again and again.

Burt Manning of J. Walter Thompson, one of the world's largest advertising agencies, started in the business as a copywriter. He became the only "creative person" ever to head the company, which has produced campaigns for such major clients as Ford, Lever Brothers, Nestle, Kellogg, Kodak, Goodyear, and Warner-Lambert.

Yes, talent and creativity are vital in a business as competitive as advertising, but without hard, well-focused, and persistent work, all that talent and creativity can come to naught. It's a lesson Manning learned firsthand, early in his career.

He came up with what he thought was a great campaign for his first big client. The client was Schlitz and the slogan Manning was urging was one that would become as famous as "Mmm-mmm good": "When you're out of Schlitz, you're out of beer." Manning was high on the campaign, but hard as this is to believe today, the Schlitz Brewing Company was not. The Schlitz people considered the whole idea too negative. They wanted Manning to come up with something more upbeat.

Manning wasn't about to give up. He went back to the customer again and again, presenting the campaign a total of six times. He recalls the final reaction: "I was able to bring it back so many times essentially because I had a relationship with this client that permitted me to and didn't make him throw me out of the room. On the sixth time he said, 'All right. I don't really think this is right, but if you guys do, test it somewhere.'

The rest, of course is advertising history. Manning's talent and creativity dreamed up a first-rate campaign, but only his hard work and persistence delivered it to the public. Dale Carnegie articulated the principle. "Patience and perseverance," he said, "will accomplish more in this world than a brilliant dash. Remember that when something goes wrong.

"Don't let anything discourage you," he wrote. "Keep on. Never give up. That had been the policy of most of those who have succeeded. Of course, discouragement will come. The important thing is to surmount it. If you can do that, the world is yours."

What this means, in practical terms, is that you've got to remember what the basic goal is —whether it's selling an ad campaign, winning an auto race, or getting elected to the presidency of the United States. Then work single-mindedly toward that goal.

And be sure to follow through. That's not always easy. You have to train yourself to march through every step, to complete every detail of every job every time. That's what makes people more valuable to a company, more crucial to an organization, more trustworthy to their colleagues and friends—following through on every detail.

"When I walk into an office and I see a stack of return calls to be made —you know, a big stack —I think to myself, 'This guy's out of control,'" says E. Martin Gibson, chief executive officer of Corning Lab Services, Inc. "That raises a little question about your dependability, if you don't even return your calls. It's little things."

People who prove themselves dependable are given greater opportunities to show how dependable they can really be. "People know they can depend on you," Gibson says. "They ask you to do something, and they don't make a follow-up note. They know you'll do it. That's dependability. Don't be one of these flaky characters who doesn't return phone calls, who gets a memo from the chairman and doesn't know quite how to answer it and sticks it aside and forgets about it. The chairman's up there wondering, What is wrong with this bozo?"

It is in those disciplined details —hundreds and thousands of little details —that success or failure is found every day. "It's old values, like getting to an appointment early, remembering to follow through on your promises, and having pride in your work," says Joyce Harvey of Harmon Associates Corporation. "If you're doing a letter of credit, you've got to follow steps one to four. You can't skip step three. Mistakes are costly. Don't move too fast. Check your details, and stay focused."

Ross Greenburg discovered the importance of discipline and concentration that night in 1990 when Mike Tyson was knocked out by Buster Douglas. Tyson was at that point the undisputed heavyweight champion of the world. Douglas was a tough fighter, but up to the opening bell, he wasn't given much of a shot.

Greenburg is executive producer of HBO Sports. By the time of the Tyson-Douglas match, he had already produced more than one hundred title fights for television. But even for a veteran like Greenburg, concentration can sometimes be shaken by dramatic events.

As Greenburg recalls, "In about the second round, it was obvious that something was right with Douglas and very wrong with Tyson. Tyson had eaten three or four straight jabs and my announcers and I immediately pounced on the story line." So far, so good.

"In the fourth round, Douglas threw a combination that rocked Tyson, and there was a loud scream on our communication line. Everyone in our truck started realizing what we were seeing in front of us. For one of the very rare times, we were getting caught up in the sporting event rather than in our individual jobs. I can remember it vividly, and all the people that work with me will tell you the same story. When I sensed this, I said, 'Okay, everybody relax. Let's remember we have a job to do here. If you let yourself become too tied to the event, you'll lose sight of the work at hand.' That's all it took. Immediately everybody was cut off from that basic, visceral reaction to the event, and we worked our way back into the job—providing replays of the staggering combinations."

There just isn't much room for slipups on live TV. "See, if I get caught up in rooting for Douglas at that point, I won't be able to cue up my tape machines and my ads. My associate directors won't be able to cue those points so you will see that replay when the round is over, which is our job."

But Greenburg admits that even he came close to losing his focus on that memorable night. "I will never, ever forget—I will never, ever forget—the moment that Tyson hit the canvas. It was as if I were reading some historical account of heavyweight championship boxing and at that split second, I saw the page turn and I was going to the new chapter and the new heavyweight champion. I'll take that to my grave. Tyson-Douglas, and maybe there will be another event down the line. I'll just be able to say, 'I was part of that.'" Steely focus isn't important just in sports television. In the case of Dr. Scott Coyne, this same kind of focus and discipline literally made the difference between life and death.

Coyne, a radiologist who had once studied for the priesthood, was the first doctor on the scene when an Avianca Boeing 727 crashed near his home on Long Island one wretched January night. For more than an hour Coyne was the only doctor on the scene.

One by one he had to tend to the passengers' injuries. He also had to soothe their nerves. He had to do it all in just a minute or two with each person on the ground, and he had to do it without language, since most of the people on the plane were from Colombia and didn't speak any English. Coyne's Spanish didn't go much beyond "Doc-tor, doc-tor. "He made himself understood by focusing every fiber of his being, Coyne said. He found a way to make this work.

"I had a stethoscope on," he says, remembering that crazy night. "I kept saying, 'Doc-tor,' and some of them were crying and screaming. You don't know if they're screaming because they're scared or because they're broken apart. I was able to communicate by touching the faces. You could tell how bad they'd been hurt by how they looked at you.

"I had to whisper in their ears. I had to maintain my composure and hold them and try to reassure them just by my expression and by my touch and holding their faces. I was unable to get a history from anybody. You know, you can't ask them where they're hurting: How bad does it hurt? Does the back hurt? I had to literally check every patient from head to toe, and then as I went down the row, I'd find these fractures were just grotesque. I'd never seen fractures like this. Legs were literally hanging off. And you check these fractures and start IVs the best you can, and you go to the next patient and start all over and check the rib cage—by hand. They couldn't tell you. You couldn't even say, 'Point,' so they could understand what you're saying. Well, it was a surreal experience because when you're going through it, the adrenaline is so high." Focus. Intense one hundred percent focus. That's what got Coyne through.

Coyne's focus was so intense that everything peripheral was just blocked out of his mind. He discovered just how focused he had been later when he spoke about the accident at a stress-management seminar. The others in the group were describing all the mayhem you'd expect in that kind of circumstance: ambulances and fire trucks and squawking radios and screaming survivors and rescue workers yelling back and forth. Coyne heard none of it.

"What I remember is how quiet it was. It all seemed so quiet and orderly. I didn't hear anything. You had to focus so much you didn't hear. It was like a trance. All I remember is just walking in utter silence. I never heard a thing. The only thing I did hear was helicopters about an hour later. Helicopters came in to evacuate some of the injured people." Focus, the ability to ignore distractions and pursue only what is important—that's what made the difference that night and helped save all those lives.

LEADERS NEVER LOSE THEIR FOCUS. THEY KEEP THEIR EYES ON THE BIG PICTURE.

□

Chapter—13

Achieving Balance

The United States Army has discovered by repeated test: that even young men —men toughened by years of arm\ training—can march better and hold up longer if they throw down their packs and rest ten minutes of every hour. So the army forces them to do just that.

Your heart is just as smart as the U.S. Army. Your heart pumps enough blood through your body every day to fill a railway tank car. It exerts enough energy every twenty-four hours to shovel twenty tons of coal onto a platform three feet high. It does this incredible amount of work for fifty, seventy, or maybe ninety years. How can it stand it? Dr. Walter B. Cannon of the Harvard Medical School explained it to me. He said, "Most people have the idea that the heart is working all the time. As a matter of fact, there is a definite rest period after each contraction. When beating at a moderate rate of seventy pulses per minute, the heart is actually working only nine hours out of the twenty-four. In the aggregate, its rest periods total a full fifteen hours per day."

During World War II, Winston Churchill, in his late sixties and early seventies, was able to work sixteen hours a day, year after year, directing the war effort of the British Empire. A phenomenal record. His secret? He worked in bed each morning until eleven o'clock, reading reports, dictating orders, making telephone calls, and holding important conferences. After lunch he went to bed again and slept for an hour. In the evening he went to bed once more and slept for two hours before having dinner at eight. He didn't cure fatigue. He didn't have to cure it. He prevented it.

Because he rested frequently, he was able to work on, fresh and fit until long past midnight.

—DALE CARNEGIE

Monsignor Tom Hartman has been a priest for more than twenty years. His whole life is dedicated to the service of God and others. His days consist of consoling the needy, ministering to the sick, advising the distraught, and trying to bring people closer to God. But one thing was sadly missing from the monsignor's busy days.

One morning his father phoned at the rectory. In those days Hartman was assigned to St. James Parish in Seaford, Long Island. His father owned a liquor store down the road in Farmingdale. In all his years of growing up and in all his time as a priest, Hartman could never remember his parents saying anything negative about him. But on the phone that morning, his father's voice had a slightly irritated tone.

"Tom, I'd like to sit down and talk with you about something," his father said.

"Sure," Hartman told him, and the two men made a date.

When they finally got together, his father spoke immediately about what was on his mind. "Tom," he said, "your mother and I admire you. We're always hearing about the good work you are doing, and we're very proud of you. But I think you're overlooking your family. I understand you've got to help a lot of people in your life, but many of those people are going to come and go. Your family will always be there for you. And what's happened is, when you call us, you're always asking us to do something for you. You just seem too busy to take the time to talk."

Hartman was momentarily taken aback. "Well, Dad," he said, "when I was growing up, I watched you. You were in the produce business working seventy hours a week. And I have to say I admired you. So you know, I've tried to do the same."

But his father didn't sound convinced. "What you don't see, Tom, is that your work is harder than mine was," he said. "Mine was physical. It was fruit and produce. And then I would come home and be present with my family." Hartman didn't know what to say, and he felt relieved when his father said he wasn't really looking for any instant response. "I just want you to think about this," his father said.

Hartman was disturbed enough by the conversation to cancel the rest of his appointments for the day. Then he decided to call his brothers and sisters. He described later what he discovered on the phone. "When I called them," he said, "we were into the conversation about three or four minutes, and every one of them said almost the exact same thing: 'What do you want?' That's when I had to admit that my father was right."

Even a man whose calling is to maintain perspective and balance needed to have someone remind him that—in one part of part of his life, at least—he wasn't practicing what he preached. That's a mistake everyone makes from time to time.

It is vital for all of us to balance out our lives, to make room for things other than work. This won't only produce happier and more satisfying personal lives. Almost inevitably, it will also make people more energetic, more focused, and more productive at work.

Walter A. Green, the chairman of Harrison Conference Services, likens a balanced, productive life to a "several-legged stool." Too many people, Green believes, have only a single dimension to their lives. They are focused round the clock on their careers.

"In my experience, all too often, this one-dimensional perspective continues throughout one's life," Green says. "What I would urge is that your life be a several-legged stool, with a dimension for your family, another for your friends, your avocations, your health. I have seen many examples of people in their thirties, forties, and fifties whose professions or careers did not materialize as they had expected. This spells trouble for those whose lives have been a one-legged stool."

This is a problem even for highly successful people. "At some stage in your life," Green continues, "you will want something else. It is possible to begin to develop friendships and interests after middle age. But watch a fifty-year-old learn to ride a bicycle for the first time!" It's not a graceful sight.

The importance of balance-to individuals and to the companies that employ them—is only now being fully understood. But well-led companies everywhere are trying to help their people put true balance into their lives.

At the New York City headquarters of Tiger Management Corporation, a worldwide money-management firm, a fully equipped workout room has been installed right outside the president's office. All Tiger employees are encouraged to use it.

"The gym is going to be tripled in size," Tiger president Julian H. Robertson, Jr., says proudly. "I find the young people all seem to come here after work. The fact that they are here rather than at health clubs all over the city is a tremendous boon for us. They are talking with each other. They are exchanging ideas. All that is really good for us." And obviously it's good for them too — physically and mentally.

"I don't think it's possible to be a great manager or a great executive without being a total person," says Andres Navarro, president of SONDA, S.A., a Chilean computer-systems company that does business in North and South

America. Navarro has an apt analogy. "If you want to be an athlete, maybe to throw the javelin, it's not enough to have the strongest arm. You need the whole body to be strong."

And if you want to be a great leader, you need all parts of your life to be strong and intact. "You see," explains Navarro, "a good executive who makes great decisions and makes money in the company but doesn't get along with his wife, his children, and other people in general is missing a crucial part of life. If you want to grow and be a good leader, you've got to be a complete man—or a complete woman. And the most important part of it is your family."

Richard Fenstermacher of the Ford Motor Company promotes the very same idea among his employees. "We tell our people, 'Your lives are two-dimensional,'" Fenstermacher says. "If you find all of your identity at Ford, that's going to be a problem because you have a responsibility to your family as well."

Undeniably, most modern leaders don't achieve a perfect balance all of the time. The many balls that are being juggled aren't easy to keep aloft. The usual tendency for ambitious people is to put the business first. It just seems so much more urgent, so much more pressing, so much more crucial.

Fred Sievert at New York Life has a different set of pressures on his time, but he admits candidly that he too finds it hard to manage all the competing interests in his life. "I'm struggling every day to bring balance into my life," he says. "I could literally spend all my waking hours at work and a year from now not know everything I'd like to know. It's very difficult."

Yes, it is. Attaining a reasonable division of time between work and leisure "is the greatest challenge," believes Ray Stata, of Analog Devices, Inc. But it's worth the effort to master the challenge.

John B. Robinson, Jr., of Fleet Financial Group, Inc., has realized the benefits that come with having a happy home life. "There has never been any doubt in my mind what's most important to me," says Robinson. A big title? Salary? Stock options? A country home? "What's most important to me, long-term, is myself, my wife, and my family."

What does this mean in practice? "I try to keep a sense of what's fair and what's equitable, and if I've been giving too much to the job and not enough to the family, I say, 'I'm not going to do that. I'm not going to say yes to that dinner, and I'm not going to shortchange my family life.'"

Most people, if they were asked directly, would probably echo Robinson's sentiments. Family is more important. Time to play is essential. But most people don't put that concept into action. They don't treat balance as a top priority. They fall into the habit of responding to the immediate pressure of work and ignoring the immediate and long-term pleasure that flows from having a satisfying personal life.

After his revelation about his family life, Monsignor Tom Hartman taught himself how to "waste" time. "I try in my life for an hour a day to do nothing," Hartman explains. "I waste time with God, with people, with nature, my job. It has transformed my eyes. Now I see the connection we have to each other. It is so important not to force things but to appreciate them." Appreciate your family, your friends, your environment, yourself, whatever it is that gets your mind off work.

At Michael and Nancy Crom's home outside San Diego, Saturdays are always reserved for that. As Nancy grabs a few last minutes of sleep, Michael and daughter Nicole make pancakes, Nicole's favorite meal. The two of them go out to the garden, where they check on the strawberry plants, water the flowers, and feed the birds. He tells her stories from the life of Nicky-Nicole and Belinda Mcintosh, the make-believe characters the two of them have invented.

"We do that every Saturday, whether I've been traveling or I've been in the office," Michael says. "Watching the joy in her eyes keeps me joyful too."

Wolfgang Schmitt of Rubbermaid takes a walk with his family most nights. "It would be unusual if we didn't go out for a walk," Schmitt explains. "If our older sons are there, they go with us. The little guy always goes with us because he lives at home. We go out for forty minutes, an hour, whatever, just walking around. We do it no matter what the weather."

Schmitt also makes a point of spending time alone. "Just physically doing something is therapy. Raking leaves, cutting wood, planting trees. Any chore is therapeutic."

Bill Makahilahila at SGS-Thomson makes time for himself every day—even though it means getting up at three o'clock in the morning. Makahilahila explains his practice of predawn rising: "I'm busy all day. I'm usually here until seven or eight in the evening, and I know I need to be here in the morning. I don't know why, but I've just gotten to the point where I am in deep meditation in the mornings. It's so quiet, I can stretch myself, be creative, read, or reflect on my day."

The benefits are immediate. "When I've done that," he says, "I begin to have peace of mind and self-confidence, even in the midst of the deepest problems that I know I'm going to have to face that day."

Coming's David Luther runs. He also vacations with his wife and son four times a year, skiing or beach combing. He makes sure he reads things that have nothing to do with work, and when all else fails, "I just go out and sit on the deck and watch the hawks."

Once you've analyzed how to enjoy your leisure time, bring some of that same spirit into work. Who ever said the office has to be a depressing place?

Certainly not Richard Fenstermacher of the Ford Motor Company. Fenstermacher recalls doing business with a company that brought that spirit of levity right into the executive suite. "When they bring somebody on the board," explains Fenstermacher, "they give the new person a Mickey Mouse watch. There's a big presentation out of the office. Everybody comes and stands around, and somebody gives a speech. The thing is, you don't have to spend twenty-five years with this company to get a watch. Here's your watch. When you look at that watch, we want to remind you to have fun when you work. That's why it's Mickey Mouse."

Tom Saunders makes enjoyment a high priority at his international merchant bank, Saunders Karp & Company. "We waste time. When we've got a little bit of time to sit around, we laugh at each other about something or make fun of each other. I make fun of them all the time and they make fun of me worse. But all the time I'm ragging them, all the time. We have good times. We don't take ourselves too seriously."

Television newsman Hugh Downs has borrowed Churchill's time-tested method of workday relaxation and given it his own special spin. "The one thing I have in common with great people—only one thing— is that I can sleep for very short periods and be refreshed," says Downs. "I can sit down in a chair and go to sleep for three minutes, five minutes, and wake up and it's like I've had a night's sleep. I would go into my dressing room often when I was otherwise all ready and say, 'Wake me two minutes before air time,' And they'd come in and wake me two minutes before air. I'd go out and do the show.

"My wife laughs at that," Downs continues. "She says, 'If you were condemned to death in two hours, you're going before the firing squad in two hours, you'd take a nap the first hour and face the problem the second hour.' It's probably true. If there were nothing I could do about it in that first hour, it would be appropriate to take a nap."

What is always appropriate—at the office, at home, on the road, wherever you happen to find yourself—is to keep real balance in your life. As Fleet Financial's John Robinson says, "There are many ways of getting involved in outside activities. Every time you get involved in outside interests, it adds balance— whether it's church-related, civic-related, or school-related. I just try to avoid extremes, I guess."

Singer-songwriter Neil Sedaka had two close friends growing up in Brooklyn, a young couple who had great ambition in their lives but also just loved to have a good time. Over the years they both achieved tremendous professional and financial success, but they lost something along the way. It was the balance they once knew in their lives. Sedaka wrote a song about his friends, which turned into a giant hit. The song was called "The Hungry Years."

"They struggled to hit the top," Sedaka recalls. "Success and money. But when they finally did it, they discovered that they missed the times when they were just getting started, when they were hanging out in the old neighborhood, when they were building a life together.

"It's like, 'I want that five-million-dollar home.' But then you finally hit it, you actually get to move in, and after a couple of months, you say, 'Is this all? Is this it?' You miss those years that you did things together. You've lost some of the pleasure and balance in your life." There's nothing wrong with material success, but that alone is not enough to sustain a happy life.

How can you start balancing your life? The first step is to change your attitude. You've got to stop thinking of time for your family, for exercise, or for leisure as wasted time. Achievers often feel they need to apologize for leisure time. Try to rid yourself of that thought. Relaxation is not a dirty word.

This leads to the second step in the process: you have to make time for leisure activity. Most of us are over committed.

Perhaps it's time to reevaluate priorities. Make a decision to devote as much energy to planning your leisure time as you devote to planning your workday.

The third step is to act. Do something. Get involved in activities that are not work-related. They will leave you happier, healthier, more focused, and as a result, a better leader.

CONSISTENTLY HIGH PERFORMANCE COMES FROM A BALANCE BETWEEN WORK AND LEISURE.

□

Chapter—14

Creating a Positive Mental Attitude

I was asked once on a radio program to tell in three sentences the most important lesson I ever learned. That was easy. "The most important lesson I have ever learned," I said, "is the stupendous importance of what we think. If I knew what you think, I would know what you are, for your thoughts make you what you are. By changing our thoughts, we can change our lives."

I now known with a conviction beyond all doubt that the biggest problem you and I have to deal with—in fact, almost the only problem we have to deal with—is choosing the right thoughts. If we can do that, we will be on the high road to solving all our problems. The great philosopher who ruled the Roman Empire, Marcus Aurelius, summed it up in eight words, eight words that can determine your destiny: "Our life is what our thoughts make it."

Yes, if we think happy thoughts, we will be happy. If we think miserable thoughts, we will be miserable. If we think fear thoughts, we will be fearful. If we think sickly thoughts, we probably will be ill. If we think failure, we will certainly fail. If we wallow in self-pity, everyone will want to shun us and avoid us.

Am I advocating a Pollyanna attitude toward all our problems? No. Unfortunately, life isn't that simple. But

I am advocating—in the strongest of terms —that we assume a positive attitude instead of a negative one.

—DALE CARNEGIE

Denis Potvin was the most hated man in Madison Square Garden. From the moment he skated onto the ice that night, the New York Islanders' captain was assaulted with a roar of boos. And that's not all he was assaulted with.

Madison Square Garden was the home arena for the Islanders' archrivals, the New York Rangers hockey team. Potvin's power on the ice, his outspoken personality, and his pyrotechnic skating style had turned him into the player that Ranger fans most loved to hate.

"It got so bad my teammates didn't know what to do," Potvin recalls. "In the dressing room before we went out, a few of them would try to say, 'Well, let's go out and beat them tonight.' You could see people starting to say something. Then they'd just be quiet. What do you say to a guy who is the most hated person in the building for the next two and a half hours?" Most of Potvin's fellow Islanders said nothing.

"I remember one night, standing on the blue line right before the game began," he says. "In those days, they used to dim the lights for the National Anthem. They would bring out a singer and put a spotlight on the singer and the flag." They don't do that before hockey games at Madison Square Garden anymore. That night is the reason why.

"I was standing there," Potvin recalls. "I had taken my helmet off like I always did. And the fans started throwing things. I heard something go by my ear. It sent shivers right through my body. I didn't know what it was, but I was scared. I was really, really scared. When the lights came back up, I skated over and looked. It was a nine-volt battery, one of those big round ones, hurled from somewhere up above." It could easily have hit Potvin in the head. At that moment this hockey titan had a choice. He could let himself become overwhelmed by all the hostility.

There were literally thousands of people shouting their hatred at him. He could let the fear and anger chase him off the ice, or he could play in front of this angry and possibly dangerous crowd.

Potvin chose to play. He stood up to the arena full of hostility and turned those cowardly threats into a personal challenge. He fed off all that negative energy and used it to fuel an incredible, positive strength. All of this was accomplished right in Denis Potvin's mind.

"It was almost a blessing," he says, looking back on that hostile night. "I played very well in the Garden that night. And from that point on, I always played very well in the Garden. I was motivated beyond belief because the only way I could answer these people was by winning in the Garden.

"When I had the puck, they'd boo me. When I shot the puck in the net, they'd boo me. When I hit a player, they'd boo me. And I started to love it. I really did. All of a sudden, it became something bigger than me. And Madison Square Garden was the only place in the whole National Hockey League where, the minute I walked into the building, I was ready to play.

"There was Goliath, and here I was, little David, sitting on the middle of the ice. But I was more in control than anybody in that building. I was going to exercise that control. I would play my heart out in the Garden every time."

Mental attitude. The power we hold in our heads. The way reality can be changed dramatically by a single, solitary thought.

It sounds a little hard to believe. "Think happy thoughts, and you will be happy. Think successful thoughts, and you will succeed." Or from the ice at Madison Square Garden, "Convert that huge wall of hostility into a source of positive strength." Did Dale Carnegie and Denis Potvin go skating off the deep end together? Hardly. Both of them knew the power of attitude. The old expression had it wrong: it isn't what you eat that determines what you are. You are what you think.

Contrary to what most people want to believe, outside influences do not usually determine personal happiness. What matters is how we react to those influences, good or bad.

Marshall and Maureen Cogan achieved great financial and professional success. He was a partner at a big New York investment-banking firm. She was a rising star in the publishing business, who would become editor-in-chief of Art & Auction magazine. Their three children were all in private school and doing well. The Cogans had a beautiful co-op apartment in the city, and they had just built a summer home in East Hampton. It was a big, modern place near the ocean, and people came literally from around the world to see this unusual home. The house won several architecture and design awards. It was featured in more than one national magazine. And the Cogan children seemed to love that house as much as their parents did.

Then trouble arrived. Marshall, who had been growing bored at the investment firm, decided to strike out on his own. Despite his high expectations and the encouragement of his colleagues and friends, Marshall's new business never really got off the ground. His timing turned out to have been miserable —right at the start of a recession. Almost overnight, the business Marshall had sunk all his savings in was worthless, and the income he was expecting had disappeared. All this bad luck was topped off by one final blow: just at the most crucial point of his struggles to keep the business afloat, Marshall came down with hepatitis, which confined him home to bed for more than a month.

Marshall's bankers were full of personal empathy, but they wouldn't budge an inch in their demand: "You'll have to sell the new house." He couldn't stand the idea.

It was hard to break the news to his wife. He had no idea how she—or the children—would react. He needn't have worried. "Then we'll sell the house, that's it," said Maureen.

So the Cogans sold their house, along with every last piece of furniture in it. All they would have to do was pack their clothes, collect the children's toys, turn out the lights, and lock the door.

"Look, we should take the kids out to the house," Maureen told Marshall the day before the new owners were set to arrive. "We can give each one of them a big trash bag to put all their toys in, and we can bring all that stuff back to the city."

Marshall wasn't so sure. "I don't want the children to see it," he said. "I don't want them to be a part of this. You and I will do it."

"No way," Maureen told him. "They're going to come. They're going to see what it is to be down. They're going to understand, because they're going to watch you come back, and they're going to understand that if that happens to them one day, they can come back too."

So the parents agreed. Everyone piled into the car, and they rode out to East Hampton. The children cleaned out their rooms, while the parents collected the clothes and a few other personal effects. When it came time to leave, they all stood together for a moment on the front steps of the house, and then Marshall locked the door.

Then the five of them climbed back in the car for the drive to the city. That's when Maureen spoke quietly to Marshall. "We'll put this in perspective," she said. "So we're not going off to the Caribbean. So we're not running off to our house in East Hampton. Life will go on."

And then she talked to the kids as well. "No, we don't have our house," she said. "But we have a nice apartment. We're together. Daddy's healthy, and he's going to start a new business. Everything's going to be fine."

It was, The children didn't have to change schools. They even made it to summer camp that year. Soon enough, Marshall was back in business and doing well. More important than all of that, a lesson had been learned, a lesson that showed up again almost twenty years later.

Explains Maureen, "My oldest son had a failure. He started a business that we had to close down so it would not go into bankruptcy. It was a tough, public failure for him, and he was very young, just twenty-five, I remember saying to him, 'How are you doing?' And he said, 'It's awful. I've got a few more months before I'm closed.' He didn't want to go bankrupt; he wanted to pay off his debts, close the business, and leave.

"But then he said, 'I remember the time it happened to Daddy, and I'll be fine. I will get through this. I know I can do this because I watched, and I remember.'"

So how do you develop that kind of outlook? How do you change your reactions to those outer forces?

Make it a conscious priority. Think about it every day. "When you put your feet on the floor in the morning," explains Stanley R. Welty, Jr., president of the Wooster Brush Company, "you'll make it a good day or a bad day by controlling your thought processes. We're either going to enjoy life that day or we're not.

"And with all due respect to the external forces we all face in life and business every day, even under the most frustrating situations, you get to decide in large measure what kind of day it will be. So you laugh at the situation, if you have to. There are times you just throw up your hands, and you laugh."

Humor is vital. Never forget that this simple element helps maintain perspective. Welty agrees. "Keep it in perspective," he advises. "When things don't seem to be going well, relax, take your time. Think about what's going on and your reaction to it. Tell yourself, Back up ten yards, and see how we go at the next play."

There are hundreds of things that can irritate, worry, or annoy you. Don't let them. Don't let the small things get you down. "When you get cut off on the freeway, there are only two things you can do," says Ted Owen, publisher of the San Diego Business Journal, who like most Southern Californians spends an awful lot of time behind the wheel. "You can swear at the other driver and give some obscene gesture, or you can shrug and say to yourself, 'How long is it going to take this guy to end up in the junk heap? He's not going to make it to work the way he's driving.'"

Neither approach will have much effect on how quickly you arrive at the office. Shrugging at this trivial irritation will get you there in a much happier and more productive frame of mind. It might even add a couple of years to your life.

Owen wasn't born with this laissez-faire outlook on life. He used to have one of those high-tension personalities, but he came over the years to recognize how self-destructive it could be. When he was asked to run the Business Journal, where he would be commenting frequently on how other executives perform, he decided he'd better overcome his own attitude problems.

"Many of us tend to be reactive and over reactive," he observes. "Since starting this job, I've never been angry at work. I got angry other places, but I haven't been angry here." People are responding like they've never responded before.

After years of struggle, things were finally looking up for Mary Kay Ash. She had remarried. The children were finally grown. She and her new husband had saved just enough money to start a small cosmetics company, a dream she had nurtured for years.

Then her dream nearly disintegrated. "The day before we were to open this company," Ash recalls, "my husband died of a heart attack right there at the breakfast table. My husband was to handle the administration of the company. I don't know a thing about administration, even today. Every single penny was committed. We had only five thousand dollars, my personal savings. It sounds like very little, but probably it would be worth fifty thousand today. "On the day of the funeral, we had no time to waste. My two sons and my daughter and I sat down to decide what to do. Do I stop or do I go on? All my dreams just plunged to the ground."

But Mary Kay Ash believed in herself too much to give up. Her son Richard, who was just twenty, offered to do what he could. "Mother," he said, "I'll move to Dallas to help you."

She had her doubts. "I thought, 'Big deal/ How would you like to turn your life savings over to a twenty-year-old? I figured maybe he could lift boxes I couldn't. I didn't know if he could fill out an order or not. I mean, he had been just one kid that I had to bring up by myself."

But Ash wasn't one to let doubt overwhelm her. She doesn't take well to defeat. So she pressed on. "That was the beginning of the company. True to his word, Richard moved to Dallas the very next day with his little two-month bride on his arm. The lawyers were saying, 'Why don't you go directly to the trash and throw the money in, because you're never going to make it.' And pamphlets from Washington told us how many cosmetics companies go broke every morning."

Her positive attitude got her through it all. She just kept telling herself, "I think that people will support that which they have to create. I think it can be done, and I'm going to try." With an attitude like that, is it any surprise that Ash succeeded?

These positive, self-confident feelings don't only help you achieve more. They also make other people want to be associated with you. We all respond to the attitudes of others. That's why people are drawn to those with upbeat outlooks on life. We want to surround ourselves with friends or coworkers who are happy and productive, who have a can-do, it's-no-problem attitude. Just as predictably, the constant complainer in any crowd doesn't get much company.

Why is this? Attitude rubs off on others, good or bad. This is a vital concept to remember for anyone who wants to be a successful leader today. There are few more powerful motivators than a positive attitude.

We all know organizations where a large percentage of the employees are unhappy. How did they get that way? Slowly, one employee at a time. A leader has to fight that spread, constantly substituting positive feelings and attitudes for negative ones.

David Luther, the quality chief at Corning, Incorporated, learned about the importance of focusing on the positive — and ignoring the negative—from a smart union leader in Detroit, a man who represented workers at a factory that made Lincolns and Thunder-birds.

"An enormous place, it had been very successful in quality," Luther says. "This guy got up and said, I made the change when I started worrying about the ninety percent who said yes instead of the ten percent who said no.' That's a very insightful statement because a lot of labor negotiations revolve around the ten percent who are always resisting. People are always saying, 'Well, let's convert them.' This guy knew better. He said, "That's the wrong way. I'm going to work with the ninety percent who want to move forward.' And that's what he did, a very insightful approach."

Luther has developed this philosophy at Corning. "Eventually," he says, "I may win some of the others over, yes. But these ninety percent are ready to come along. They're sitting out there with the power doors open. They're waiting, and the motor's running. You don't want to be locked in here trying to convince these last people when the vast majority are waiting outside, ready to climb on board."

One of a leader's most important jobs, then, is to set a positive, self-confident tone, showing others that failure isn't even a possibility.

When Julius Caesar sailed across the channel from Gaul and landed with his legions in what is now England, what did he do to ensure the success of his army? A very clever thing: he halted his soldiers on the chalk cliffs of Dover. Looking down to the waves two hundred feet below, the men could see every one of the ships that had carried them across the channel— completely ablaze.

So here these soldiers were, stranded in the enemy's country, their last link with the Continent entirely severed, their last means of retreat going up in smoke. What else could they do but advance? What else could they do but conquer? What else could they do but fight with every ounce of strength that was buried in their souls? That is precisely what they did.

A positive attitude isn't important only in life-or-death struggles like this, where the soldiers' attitude was infused by desperation. It's also the secret to building a happy life and a successful career. It is the cornerstone of leadership.

That's what Hugh Downs believes, at least. "You really don't have to be unkind," says Downs, the veteran ABC newsman and program host. Downs recalls a man he worked with in television—an aggressive, hyper ambitious TV man on the make. "He was almost pathological. He sought to climb by taking advantage of other people and what I call 'kicking open doors.'"

The man did make some initial progress advancing his career, but the people he alienated, the people he abused, the people he disrespected during his single-minded climb—they did not forget. They resented him with a passionate unanimity. When he stumbled, as all of us will from time to time, these people simply stepped aside and let him fall.

"I have never once kicked open a door of opportunity," Downs says. So how then did he get so far? Instead of aggressive ambition, he substituted patience and a keen attentiveness. "You need to be alert," he observes, "so that if the door ever opens, you can dart right through. If you kick a door open, it's apt to come swinging back and hit you in the face. This has happened two or three times to this man I was talking about. I've always believed you don't do it that way, but you have to be alert to take advantage of whatever opportunity there is." In the long run, his attitude has more than paid off for Downs, and it's made the people he's worked with push for his success. "One of the things I cherish most," Downs says, "is something Tom Murphy gave to me." Murphy was chairman of Capital Cities ABC. "I don't remember what the occasion was. I guess it was my fiftieth anniversary in broadcasting. He gave me a clock with an inscription that said—and it sounds outrageously flattering—but it said, 'Nice guys don't finish last.'

"I thought it was a very kind thing for the people here to say. The sentiment is true, and I feel sorry for people who think they have to abandon a civilized approach to the world in order to be successful. If that kind of technique brings any success, it's usually temporary. In the end, it's very painful, and you build an awful lot of enemies on the way up." And you won't enjoy the climb.

GAIN STRENGTH FROM THE POSITIVE AND DON'T BE SAPPED BY THE NEGATIVE.

□

Chapter—15

Learning Not to Worry

Many years ago, a neighbor rang my doorbell one evening and urged me and my family to be vaccinated against smallpox. He was only one of thousands of volunteers who were ringing doorbells all over New York City. Frightened people stood in lines for hours at a time to be vaccinated. Vaccination stations were opened not only in all hospitals, but also in firehouses, police precincts, and in large industrial plants. More than two thousand doctors and nurses worked feverishly day and night, vaccinating crowds. Eight people in New York City had smallpox—and two had died. Two deaths out of a population of almost eight million.

Now, I had lived in New York for many, many years, and no one had ever yet rung my doorbell to warn me against the emotional sickness of worry—an illness that, during the same time period, had caused ten thousand times more damage than smallpox.

No doorbell ringer had ever warned me that one person out of ten now living in these United States will have a nervous breakdown—induced in the vast majority of cases by worry and emotional conflicts. So I am writing this chapter to ring your doorbell and warn you.

Please take to heart the words of Dr. Alexis Carrel: "Those who do not know how to fight worry die young."

—DALE CARNEGIE

In the years since Dale Carnegie wrote that, we have learned to treat—even to prevent—many of the diseases that worried people most. No doubt in the years to come we will cure many of the diseases that worry us today. But as for the crippling disease of worry, we seem to have made almost no progress at all. It ravages have only grown worse.

Nowhere is this more true than in today's volatile business world. Layoffs, buyouts, and corporate restructurings. Downsizings, cutbacks, and sudden invitations to clean out your desk. Retrenchments. Outplacements. Pare backs. Some days you need a whole new dictionary just to keep the euphemisms straight. And if that's not enough to cause an ulcer or two, how does "cost containment" sound? Or "hostile takeover?"

Companies that were once considered solid as redwoods are being shaken to their very roots. Countless others—big names from the annals of business history —have been chopped up and carried away. Whole layers of middle management vaporized: what middle manager wouldn't worry about that? Companies shedding divisions the way snakes shed their scales: what division chief wouldn't be concerned? A brand-new breed of corporate raider, looking lustfully for companies with extra fat: what well-ensconced executive wouldn't feel a nervous twinge?

Yes, changes were necessary. Some of them were long overdue. The clear-eyed truth is this: companies that don't stay lean and competitive, that aren't creative and flexible, that don't move quicker than the competition—those are the dinosaurs of today. And their futures are just about as bright.

But change causes anxiety. Change causes stress. It makes people nervous. It makes them concerned. Of course it does. Many of the assumptions that were once considered unshakable —assumptions that people built their professional lives around—turn out not to be so unshakable anymore. It's only natural to feel a little insecure. It used to be that most of the patients who walked into Dr. Marvin Frogel's psychiatric office wanted to talk about problems they were having at home— anger with the spouse, frustration with the children, resentment over how they were raised. Obviously, people are still concerned about those issues. But far more of Frogel's patients today are racked with worry over what is happening at work.

"People are terrified they're going to lose their jobs," says Dr. Frogel, who practices in Great Neck, New York. "That's something I never saw before. People are walking in the door literally quaking about what will happen at work.

"You get one shakeout, and then everyone is waiting for the other shoe to drop. And it's not just two shoes, it's twenty shoes. People get fired. Then come the early-retirement programs. Then the layoffs. People don't know if they're going to have a job the next day."

"Look at IBM," says Earl Graves, editor of Black Enterprise magazine. In recent years the once-invincible computer giant has experienced major cutbacks, as its dominance was challenged by smaller companies in America and abroad.

"It doesn't mean they will never come back. But when they're laying off people in Poughkeepsie, IBM will never be the same company again. That's turmoil, and that's when you've got to say, 'Where's your happiness going to be?' People who are leaving IBM are finding out that life is not over. When you think your wings have been clipped, you'll find out you can still fly. You think, leaving IBM, you can't fly out of the nest, but you can."

When Dale Carnegie first turned his attention to the subject of worry, the world was still gripped by the Great Depression. He could see the jagged lines of worry on the faces of his students and friends.

"As the years went by," Carnegie wrote, "I realized that worry was one of the biggest problems that adults had to face. A large majority of my students were businessmen—executives, salesmen, engineers, accountants, a cross section of all the trades and professions—and most of them had problems. There were women in the classes—businesswomen and housewives. They had problems too. Clearly, what I needed was a textbook on how to conquer worry. So I tried to find one.

"I went to New York's great public library at Fifth Avenue and Forty-second Street and discovered to my great astonishment that this library had only twenty-two books listed under the title Worry. I also noticed, to my amusement, that it had one hundred eighty-nine books listed under Worms. Almost nine times as many books about worms as about worry ! Astounding, isn't it?

"Since worry is one of the biggest problems facing humanity, you would think, wouldn't you, that every high school and college in the land would give a course on how to stop worrying? Yet if there is even one course on that subject in any college in the land, I have never heard of it."

Carnegie spent seven years reading and studying about worry. He interviewed all the leading experts of the day. He read every worry book he could get his hands on, most of which turned out to be dense, psychiatric treatises or for some other reason inadequate as practical guides. Carnegie did more than read and study, though. He relied on what he called his "laboratory for conquering worry"—the adult-education classes he was teaching most nights.

Out of all that research came a book about worry and stress: How to Stop Worrying and Start Living, published in 1944. For the first time ever, the basic techniques for overcoming worry were laid out in a simple, straightforward way. These techniques have been updated and revised many times over the years, as new causes for worry have presented themselves.

Learn these techniques. Apply them every day. Almost certainly, you will gain greater control over your life. You will experience less stress and worry. You will end up mentally and physically healthier too.

LIVE IN DAY-TIGHT COMPARTMENTS.

Business was slow at Chase Manhattan Financial Services in San Diego, California. The loan department was already $9 million behind on the year. The people who worked in the department were growing increasingly tense with each other. And Becky Connolly, the loan-office manager, was so worried she could barely sleep at night.

Then she decided to try living in day-tight compartments. "Listen," she told the staff. "This has always been a cyclical business. Loans have always come in waves. Just focus on your daily activities, your customer calls, servicing and following up on the advertising. We'll all get through this slump." The results? A happier, more productive work force, and soon enough loan activity picked up.

It's mind-boggling to think about how much energy gets wasted on the future and on the past. The past is over, and the future hasn't yet arrived. Try as we might, we are utterly unable to affect either one. There's only one time we can possible live in. That time is the present. That time is today.

"You and I," Dale Carnegie wrote, "are standing this very second at the meeting place of two eternities: the vast past that has endured forever, and the future that is plunging on to the last syllable of recorded time. We can't possibly live in either of those eternities—no, not even for one split second. But by trying to do so, we can wreck both our bodies and our minds. So let's be content to live the only time we can possibly live: from now until bedtime."

Remember this, and don't go crazy worrying about what might have been. Don't get all tied up in anxiety about things that may or may not happen at some future time. Focus your attention instead on the one place where you can do any good—the reality of life today.

So give up the wallowing, and give up the butterflies. Sure, think about tomorrow and learn from yesterday. Plan ahead and try to improve upon the experiences of the past. But while you're doing all that, remember that the future and the past are the two things nobody can possibly change.

Singer-songwriter Neil Sedaka learned this truism from his mother. "She always said, 'Take each day as a gift. Try to live with the good and the bad, looking more at the good.'"

Is that easy? "It's a constant struggle," Sedaka agrees, "but I think it can be done. We all have our problems, and going through the day it hits us. Try to push it away. You've got to." Work in the realm of the present. Put your energy, put your attention, put your drive where it will count: today.

And then get to work. You just may be surprised by how much can be accomplished in one day-tight compartment.

As the Scottish poet Robert Louis Stevenson said, "Anyone can carry his burden, however hard, until nightfall. Anyone can do his work, however hard, for one day. Anyone can live sweetly, patiently, lovingly, purely, till the sun goes down. And this is all that life really means."

TAKE COMFORT FROM THE LAW OF AVERAGES.

Theo Bergauer could see immediately that something was wrong. Bergauer is the general manager of Karl Bergauer GmbH & Co. KG, the largest construction company in Northern Bavaria. His secretary of many years looked like she was about to cry.

"What's the matter with you?" Bergauer asked the woman.

She told him that her son had just joined the German army. "The part of the army he joined, they're the first people to go to a foreign country to help out." Problems were just then brewing in Yugoslavia, and she was worried sick that her boy was about to be sent off to his death.

Bergauer didn't quite know what to say, but he thought about odds for a minute. "What are the odds that his part of the German forces will be called to go to Yugoslavia?"

About one in a hundred, they decided.

So the two of them made an agreement. Bergauer explains, "If this one percent came into reality, then she would worry a little. But until then there was no reason to worry at all."

By asking yourself just one question—and paying attention to what the answer is—you chase a good chunk of worry from your life. The question is this: "How likely is this thing to happen, anyway?"

Most people spend far too much time worrying about things that never occur. In fact, most of the things that most people worry about don't happen. That's worth remembering. "My life," wrote the French philosopher Montaigne, "has been full of terrible misfortunes, most of which never happened."

One useful trick is to try placing mathematical odds on the things that you worry most about. That's what business writer Harvey Mackay has done for most of his life. "Once you know the facts and put a probability on them," Mackay says, "you can see the situation in its proper perspective."

The odds that this airplane will crash: maybe one in one hundred thousand. That you will get fired some time this year: maybe one in five hundred, one in a thousand. The odds are probably even smaller than that. The odds that you will dump a cup of coffee on your desk: okay, maybe one in a hundred. But who really cares about that?

"So if somebody's opening up a rival business across the street, okay, sounds terrible," Mackay says. "But wait a minute. It's going to take them three years to get the equipment. We've been here thirty-two years, and we've got all this experience, all this know-how, and all this good will. So how likely do you think it is that they're really going to hurt us? Go ahead. Put odds on it." Probably not as much as you imagined at first.

"You can make these predictions on every single thing," Mackay points out. "Is so-and-so going out of business? Is someone else coming out of Chapter 11? What's going to happen here? What about the mayor? Who's going to get elected? Who's he going to appoint? It's such a great game to play. You're not betting your money, but it helps you put things into perspective. It keeps you sharp. It can make you very humble too."

COOPERATE WITH THE INEVITABLE.

For six years David Rutt had been a supervisor with Expediters International, a West Coast import-export firm. Then the job of import manager came open.

"Unfortunately," Rutt recalls, "I didn't get the promotion." He could have let this setback turn into bitterness. He could have lost interest in the position he did have. But he didn't. "I resolved not to worry about the past and to turn this loss into a gain," he says. "I resolved to help the new manager in any way I could during his first few difficult months on the job."

The payback? "I was recently given the position of assistant import manager," Rutt says.

Follow Rutt's advice: don't waste time and energy worrying about the things you cannot control.

"There are so many times I have had worries and tension and didn't have solutions for them," says Andres Navarro, the Chilean businessman. "What do you do when you're a teenager and you fall in love with a girl and she doesn't love you? There's no solution for it. You feel sad, and you feel turned down, but after a while, the question just disappears. You don't find a solution. You just live with it."

Every day our lives will be peppered with unpleasant realities of various sorts. Some of them we will be lucky enough or skillful enough to change. But there will always be problems that are beyond our reach.

Crime and poverty, the number of hours in a day, the fact that others have a grip on important parts of our lives—those are just immutable facts. Despite our strongest efforts, despite our most creative ideas, despite all the assistance we can muster on our behalf—despite all of that, some things we simple cannot control.

Too bad, isn't it, that we aren't all masters of the universe? And too bad that other people don't always do exactly what we would like. That's just life, and the sooner we learn to accept it, the happier and more successful we will be. That's what Mother Goose was driving at:

For every ailment under the sun There is a remedy, or there is none. If there be one, try to find it If there be none, never mind it.

The real trick is telling them apart.

Obviously, circumstances do not make us happy or unhappy. It's how we react to them. But we really don't have much choice about accepting the inevitable. The alternative is usually a life of disappointment and bitterness.

It's when we stop fighting the inevitable that we have the time, the energy, and the creativity to solve the problems that we can. "Be willing to have it so," said Henry James. "Acceptance of what has happened is the first step to overcoming the consequences of any misfortune."

PUT A STOP-LOSS ORDER ON YOUR WORRIES.

Like many hospitals, Sharp Cabrillo has been going through some difficult times. Lori England, a clinical specialist, was right in the middle of a big wave of layoffs, and she was certain she would be next. The whole situation at work was beginning to make her depressed.

But she made a decision about her life: she wasn't going to devote any more worry to the uncertainties at the hospital. She would instead start having fun at work-

She started teaching CPR. She put extra enthusiasm into other parts of her job. People started noticing her efforts especially against the glum background of everyone else.

"Who do you think will be laid off in the future?" England asks. "Someone down and worried? Or a valuable member of the team, throwing enthusiasm into everything she does?"

Try asking yourself the question that Wall Street investors ask themselves whenever the market falls: How much of a loss am I willing to take on this investment? If the market turns unexpectedly, how far will I allow this stock to fall? At what point do I just take the beating and walk away?

A stop-loss order, it's called on Wall Street. The message to the trader is, Sell the stock if it falls below a certain price. I'll eat the loss, but I'm not going to throw away my fortune on a single mistaken call.

You can follow the same system when it comes to worry. Ask yourself, How much worry is this one problem worth? Is it worth one sleepless night? Is it worth a week's worth of anxiety? Is it worth an ulcer to me? Very, very few problems should be. Decide in advance how much worry a problem is worth.

A job in a poorly run company, an employee who refuses to join team efforts, a supplier who delivers shoddy service-every one of those is a subject worthy of energy and concern. But how much? That's what you need to decide. Eventually, a time may come that you will simply have to say, "Get me a headhunter" or "Put him on probation" or "Hand me the vendor's list."

No problem is worth all the worry in the world.

KEEP THINGS IN PERSPECTIVE.

Some things aren't worth worrying about at all. They're just too tiny. Will my hair get messed up in the wind? Will my grass be greener than my neighbor's? Did the boss smile at me today? Most of the time it just doesn't matter. Yet we all know people who have turned their lives inside out over such trivialities. What a waste!

Some things in life really matter. Some things do not. You can cut your worry in half by learning to tell them apart. Golfer Chi Chi Rodriguez had this kind of perspective.

At the Northville Senior Classic, about 250 spectators had gathered to watch Rodriguez tee off. He was always known to put on an enjoyable show.

At the back of the tee box, a boy was sitting in a wheelchair. No one was paying the boy much attention, least of all the professional golfers who had preceded Rodriguez to the tee. Their minds were more likely on the tournament's $450,000 purse.

Just before he teed off, Rodriguez noticed the boy, and he walked over to say hello. Rodriguez took a golf glove from his pocket and placed it over the young boy's hand. This took considerable care, since the hand was severely malformed. Then Rodriguez autographed the glove and gave the boy a ball. By then the boy's face was filled with excitement and joy at the recognition he had just received from this star.

The crowd responded with loud applause at Rodriguez's act of kindness. Upon hearing the applause Rodriguez looked embarrassed. He held up his hands and gazed at the sky as if to say: "I don't deserve the applause. The person who is suffering and his family are the true heroes here."

Although Rodriguez was focused on the golf match, he also recognized what the larger stakes of life can be. Stepping up to help other people: that's a terrific worry-fighting technique.

FINALLY, GET BUSY

Nothing takes your mind off worry like having it occupied with something else. That's a technique professional actors need to learn in a hurry. "When you're up for a big film," says Annette Bening, who has had major roles in Bugsy, The Grifters, and other films, "the waiting period can be months. They meet you. Then they go away. They meet other people. Then they come back. They meet you again. One thing I found useful was to start working on the part. I would actually go to work.

There was one in particular that was going to take a lot of reading. So I found myself—as a way of dealing with the anxiety of not knowing what the outcome was going to be—I figured I would just work on it. In that particular instance, I didn't get the part."

But she won many others, and she got by with a lot less worry than many actors experience. "When I don't get a part, I just try to move on mentally, not dwell on it, get on to the next thing."

If you're finding yourself getting worried, take on a new project. Learn a new skill. Do something you believe in. Focus on the needs of others. Getting busy takes your mind off your own troubles. You'll also be serving others, which will make you feel better about yourself.

WHAT IF THERE IS GOOD REASON TO WORRY?

Despite all these fine worry-stopping techniques, you will still have problems in your life. All of us do. You can accept the inevitable. You can put an ironclad stop-loss order on your worries. You can remind yourself of what havoc all this worrying can cause.

But still you will have problems, and you will need to deal intelligently with them. Here's a useful three-step approach. If you'll just follow these three steps, it's amazing how much more clearly you'll see what you're dealing with.

1. Ask yourself, What's the worst that can possibly happen? Thankfully, most of our problems are, in fact, not matters of life and death. So maybe the worst that will happen is that you lose an important account. Or you're late for a meeting. Or your boss yells at you. Or you get passed over for a promotion you were hoping for. Unpleasant? Absolutely. The cause of untold worry for millions out there? No doubt. Deadly? Probably not.
2. Prepare yourself mentally to accept the worst, if necessary. This doesn't mean lying back and welcoming failure. It just means telling yourself, Yes, I suppose I could deal with that if I really have to. And the truth of the matter is that we can almost always recover—even from "the worst." It won't be any fun. There's no reason to pretend otherwise. But at the same time, losing a promotion or being reprimanded is not quite the end of the world. When we remind ourselves of this—"Hey, what's the worst that can happen?"—We'll be sure to confront the real issues in a far less hysterical frame of mind.
3. Then work calmly and methodically to improve upon the worst. Ask yourself, What can I do to make the situation better? How quickly should I act? who can be of help? After I make that first move, what are the second, third, fourth, and fifth things I should do? How can I measure the success of the steps I take?

Patty Adams, a marketing representative for TRW REDI Property Data, Inc., used that three-step approach in facing the scare of her life. "One day my phone rang," Adams explains. "It was my worst nightmare. My doctor wanted me back in his office as soon as possible to rerun and confirm the test." Uterine cancer.

"I was devastated by the fear of the unknown," she says. "Would I lose my femininity, or worse, my life? A thousand scenarios ran through my head. First things first. I got confirmation of the awful verdict, and of course, I totally collapsed inside."

Pulling herself together, she faced her fears and asked her doctor for the worst-case prognosis. It was "surgery with the loss of ability to have children."

Her heart sank. "At twenty-seven," Adams recalls, "I was too young and vital to face such a loss. But if I didn't go for treatment, I would die." Before she became hysterical, Adams got the facts.

"This has a ninety-five percent cure rate. At that point I recognized that even if I had the surgery, I would be no less alive."

For eighteen months she used drugs to fight the disease—without success. "When surgery was scheduled, I resigned myself to have faith and not let fear destroy me," she says. "I put myself in the mind-set that I could handle anything that life brought."

She had the surgery. Luckily, with a small loss of tissue, she was cured. "Four years later, I don't have any signs or irregular cells," she says. "Every day I face life anew."

TAME YOUR WORRIES AND ENERGIZE YOUR LIFE

□

Chapter—16

The Power of Enthusiasm

The first class I ever conducted was held at the 125th Street YMCA in New York City. It was a small class of fewer than ten men. One of the students, a salesman for the National Cash Register Company, made an astounding speech. He said that he had been horn and brought up in the city. But the autumn before, he had bought a country house. The house had just been built, and there was no grass and no garden. He decided that he wanted a bluegrass lawn.

During the winter, he burned hickory wood in his fireplace and sprinkled the ashes on the ground where he expected to make a lawn. "You know, I thought you had to sow seed to get bluegrass. But you don't. All you have to do is to throw hickory-wood ashes on the ground in the autumn, and bluegrass will come up in the spring."

I was astonished. I said to him, "If this is true, you have discovered what scientists have been working for in vain for centuries. You have discovered how to take dead matter and make it produce living matter. It just can't be done. Maybe bluegrass seed blew in on your land without you knowing anything about it. Or there may have been bluegrass growing there already. But one thing is sure: bluegrass won't grow from hickory-wood ashes alone."

I was so sure of myself that I was calm and casual in

my announcement. But the bluegrass man was excited. He leaped to his feet and exclaimed; "I know what I'm talking about, Mr. Carnegie. After all, I did it!"

And he went on and on and on, speaking with enthusiasm, animation, and spirit. When he finished, I said to the class, "How many believe this man can do what he says he can do?"

To my amazement, everyone in the room shot up a hand. When I asked them why they believed, practically all of them replied, "Because he seems so positive. He is so enthusiastic about himself."

—DALE CARNEGIE

If enthusiasm can cause a group of intelligent business people to ignore the basic laws of science, just imagine what it can do if someone is actually making sense.

Here is the bottom line on enthusiasm: it's infectious, and it makes people respond. This is true in the classroom, in the boardroom, and on the campaign trail. It's just as true in the ice-hockey rink. If you are not enthusiastic about an idea or a project, nobody else will ever be. If the leaders don't believe enthusiastically in the direction of a company, don't ever expect the employees or the customers or Wall Street to. The best way to get someone excited about an idea —or a project or a campaign—is to be excited yourself. And to show it.

Tommy Draffen had just taken a new job as a salesman with Culver Electronics Sales, a California importer of intercom speakers. According to the longstanding company practice, this meant one thing: Draffen was handed a list of incredibly tough prospects. There was one firm in particular that used to be a big Culver customer but had been lost years ago.

"I decided to make getting their business a personal challenge," Draffen says. "That meant convincing my company president that we could get the business back. He was not as sure as I was, but he didn't want to throttle back my enthusiasm. So he allowed me to visit the customer."

Draffen turned this account into a personal mission. He offered guaranteed pricing, reduced lead time, and better service. He assured the company's director of purchasing that Culver would do "whatever it takes to satisfy your needs."

The key to Draffen's enthusiasm came during his first face-to-face meeting with the purchasing director. He walked into the meeting with a smile on his face, and he said, "Glad to be back. We're going to make this work together."

Draffen never once thought he would not close this deal. He all but ignored the fact that his company had already lost this account. With an upbeat, enthusiastic attitude, he convinced the client that Culver was ready to serve again.

"As it turns out, the purchasing manager later told our president the only reason they were entertaining our offers was because of my enthusiasm. They gave us the order that will turn out to be half a million dollars a year."

Before another word is written on the subject of enthusiasm, let's clarify a widespread misconception once and for all. Loudness does not equal enthusiasm. Nor does pounding on the table, or jumping up and down, or acting like a fool. That's fake. It's obvious. It doesn't fool anyone. It almost always does more harm than good.

Enthusiasm is a feeling that has to come from inside. This concept is so important, it's worth saying again. Enthusiasm is a feeling that has to come from inside. It's not to be confused with boisterous hype.

It's true, increased physical movement and stronger voice projection sometimes accompany an inner feeling of enthusiasm. But people who indulge in super animation—you know, "I'm great, you're great, we're all so great today!" —Might as well wear a big I'm a Phony badge instead.

"Leadership starts out with the whole issue of integrity and credibility," says Ray Stata, the Analog Devices chairman. "So you have to be believed and believable. You have to be a person who honors his or her word, a person whom people can trust. I think those are prerequisites for open dialogue, as opposed to seeming manipulative or glad handing or insensitive or whatever."

The real enthusiasts of history understood this intuitively. Back in the 1950s, was Jonas Salk enthusiastic about creating a polio vaccine? Of course he was. He dedicated years of his life to the pursuit. Anyone who came in contact with Salk could see his enthusiasm immediately in the way his eyes lit up when he spoke about his research, in the round-the-clock sessions he led in the lab. Salk became an inspiration for two generations of scientists. Yes, the man positively exuded enthusiasm, but Salk did not rant and rave. Now he's devoting that very same enthusiasm to finding a vaccine for the HIV virus, the one that causes AIDS.

In 1969 Neil Armstrong was just as enthusiastic about walking on the moon. The enthusiasm was palpable even in his flat Ohio voice. "That's one small step for man," he said, "one giant leap for mankind." Armstrong didn't need to shout the sentence or do a little jig before climbing back to the Apollo spacecraft. But enthusiasm was obviously jampacked in Armstrong's thoughtful words.

In 1991, when General Norman Schwarzkopf led American troops in the Persian Gulf War, did he seem nonchalant? Not by a long shot. He didn't have to scream and shout at his troops to make them see he believed in their mission. You could just tell in a five-second news clip on CNN. None of these great enthusiasts was especially loud or boisterous. But they left no one wondering how they felt about their work.

True enthusiasm is made of two parts: eagerness and assurance. Be excited about something and express confidence in your ability to handle it. That's all enthusiasm takes. Have those two feelings about a company, a project, or an idea, and your enthusiasm will be dangerously contagious. You'll have it. Others will know you have it. Pretty soon, they'll have it, too. Guaranteed.

"Enthusiasm is something that always came naturally to me," says Olympic gymnast Mary Lou Retton. "I'm just a very positive person, and I've always surrounded myself with positive people. That's important for me."

That positive outlook was part of Retton's secret for getting through all the grueling training sessions she had to endure as a young world-class gymnast. "There were times when my coach, Bela Karolyi, was in a bad mood and was very strict in the gym. I would try to keep our group of four or five girls positive. But if you had one girl who was down and said, 'Gosh, I don't want to do this,' it would bring everybody down. I hated that. You could have ten people who were in the best possible mood, but if you have that one negative person, you'd bring the whole group down. So I'd try and steer away from those people."

"Always surround yourself with happy, successful people," agrees Harvey Mackay, the business-book author. "I don't go around with negative people. If your friends and your peers and the people you respect and the people that you're reading about are upbeat, enthusiastic, confident people with a lot of self-esteem, that will also become a part of you."

It is almost impossible to underestimate the power of enthusiasm. "Every great and commanding movement is the triumph of enthusiasm," Ralph Waldo Emerson once said. "Nothing great was ever achieved without it." This was true of the civil rights movement. It was true of the founding of America. It is just as true of all big companies today.

Enthusiasm is as important as high ability, as important as hard work. We all know people who are brilliant and accomplish nothing. We all know people who work hard and get nowhere. But people who work hard, love their jobs, and convey enthusiasm—those are the ones who are going places.

Dale Carnegie once asked a friend how he chose his top subordinates, the people on whose abilities his business would succeed or fail. The friend's answer might sound surprising to some. "The difference in actual skill and ability and intelligence between those who succeed and those who fail is usually neither wide nor striking," said Frederick D. Williamson, president of the New York Central Railway. "But if two people are nearly equally matched, the one who is enthusiastic will find the scales tipped in his favor. And a person who has second-rate ability with enthusiasm will often outstrip someone of first-rate ability without enthusiasm."

The chief failing of IQ tests has always been that they don't measure a person's enthusiasm or emotional drive. When these tests were first introduced two generations ago, they were touted as amazing predictive tools. By measuring someone's "intelligence quotient," you could predict with great precision what that person would be able to achieve in life, or so the IQ testing companies claimed.

If only life were as simple as that. The idea was alluring, especially at a time when the whole world was placing more of its faith in science. The standardized-testing business took off. College admissions officers relied on the tests slavishly to determine who was worth accepting. School guidance counselors used them to steer youngsters into advanced or remedial work. The military used the IQ tests to decide who was officer material and who got to clean latrines.

Sure, intelligence matters. Some people are blessed with more of it than other people, and that makes certain things easier for them. Ditto for creative talent, or athletic prowess, or perfect pitch, or any of life's other precious gifts. But this raw talent is really only half the total picture. The other half we must paint for ourselves.

Even the people at the Educational Testing Service, the New Jersey company that administers many of today's standardized tests, now go to great lengths to emphasize how incomplete their results really are. School admissions officers are warned not to interpret these results too rigidly. A whole range of other factors must apply —personal enthusiasm at the top of the list.

National Hockey League Hall-of-Famer Denis Potvin, who led the New York Islanders to four straight Stanley Cups, knows a little something about enthusiasm.

"When I got to training camp," the former Islanders captain remembered, "I needed to be emotionally excited about hockey. So I didn't take the approach that some players did, thinking I should skate all summer long. I actually felt the opposite: I didn't want to skate a lot.

"So when I got into training camp, I was never in as great shape physically as a lot of the people were. I knew I had to work extra hard to be in shape. But the thing I had over them was that I was genuinely enthusiastic about playing hockey again. Here it was, the fifteenth September of my professional career, and I felt like I was a kid again."

No, you can't fake enthusiasm. But yes— absolutely, yes—you can create it, you can nourish it, and you can put it to work for you. Dale Carnegie explained the process like this: "The way to acquire enthusiasm is to believe in what you are doing and in yourself and to want to get something definite accomplished. Enthusiasm will follow as night follows the day."

How can you get this process started? "By telling yourself what you like about what you are doing and passing on quickly from the part you don't like to the part you do like. Then act enthusiastic. Tell someone about it. Let them know why it interests you. If you act 'as if you are interested in your job, that bit of acting will tend to make your interest real. It will also tend to decrease your fatigue, your tensions, and your worries."

Enthusiasm is easiest to attain when you have real goals in your life, things you are genuinely looking forward to. Let that happen, and enthusiasm will grow inside of you. Wake up in the morning and take a minute to think about something pleasing that will happen that day. It doesn't have to be anything monumental. Maybe it's some part of your job you always enjoy. Maybe it's a friend you're meeting for lunch. Maybe it's a family outing, a beer with your friends, an hour on the squash court or in an aerobics class. Whatever the pleasing event is, what's important is this: life doesn't need to be dull or uninteresting. We all need goals and experiences worth looking forward to. These are the things that give a forward thrust to life. People who reflect on this even for a moment can build a whole new way of looking at life. They can break from the ruts that they restuck in. They will, in other words, live enthusiastically. When you do, the results can be truly remarkable.

"Modern organizations need enthusiastic leadership more than ever," believes Andres Navarro, president of Chile's SONDA, S.A. "That's almost a definition of leadership —the ability to transmit enthusiasm to other people for a common goal. If you want a group of people tomorrow or today to have enthusiasm and feel happy working on a project, it's useless to write a memo, 'Starting tomorrow everyone will have a lot of enthusiasm.'" You have to have the enthusiasm yourself.

"If you don't have enthusiasm, it's impossible you will transmit enthusiasm to anyone," Navarro says. "So if you want to change an environment, first of all you have got to change yourself. If you won't change first, you can't even change your children. If you want your son to be enthusiastic at playing soccer, you've got to be enthusiastic.

"Enthusiasm is something you transmit through your eyes, in the way you move, the way you act all day, more than the way you write it in a memo. Actually, I think all of us can have enthusiasm for something. If you don't feel any type of enthusiasm, you might as well be dead. Once you discover that you are enthusiastic in doing something, it's easy to develop the ability to get yourself enthusiastically behind almost any goal."

Indeed, having enthusiasm almost always assures success. That may be hard to believe, but the raw evidence suggests it is true.

You can tell that David Webb, the former president of Lever Brothers Company, brims with enthusiasm by just watching him walk through his office door. He's not a screamer or a grip-and-grin artist. But there's a positive, •joyful spirit in his stride, head up, a look of eagerness in his eyes. This may sound trivial, but this look has more force than most of us imagine. This is no accident.

"People are always going to read you in the elevator," Webb says. "You express whatever your values are twenty-four hours a day. People have a good memory."

Webb goes on, "I learned this from a man who became the chairman of Unilever, Sir David Orr. I took over for him in India. He was the marketing director. He knew everyone. David Orr went everywhere. We have a huge network of distributors. Every time you go to a distributor, they garland you. I toured all over India, and I tried desperately to find a distributor where David Orr hadn't been, where there wasn't some photograph of him on the wall. He knew every salesman in the country." It was Sir David's enthusiasm they all remembered.

Webb learned this lesson, and he didn't forget it as he rose through the ranks to CEO of Lever Brothers. "I'd met every salesman in this company —I think we've got about seven hundred fifty—within three months of being in the business," he recalls. "They know me. They can relate to me. I'm out there playing the fool with them sometimes, enjoying the fun, just being with them. I love the salesmen and the people in the plants. But there isn't anyone I don't like."

Thomas Doherty was an executive at Nor star Bank when the regional financial institution was acquired by Fleet Financial Group, Inc. Doherty stayed on, running all of Fleet's business for the New York City region.

Not surprisingly, many of Doherty's colleagues were extremely nervous about the change in ownership. "That's natural," Doherty says. "Customers, families, and friends are going to ask us, 'How do you feel about the merger?' If you're enthusiastic over it, then they are going to be enthusiastic. I think attitude and enthusiasm are what people are looking for. If you come to your desk every day and you have a long face, people read that immediately. But if you get on the elevator and you say good morning to everyone just as you have in the past, people notice that. They think, Gee, he's enthusiastic. Why not give it a chance?"

This prescription, of course, presupposes that there is something you like about your work. Assessing this realistically may require a little soul-searching. The truth of the matter is that there are things to like about most jobs, but let's not gloss over the hard reality: there are some jobs that are simply miserable—or simply inappropriate to your temperament, your skills, or your goals. If that condition applies to you, do something about it. You will never achieve real success if you cannot be excited by your life or your work. Many people have bounced around from job to job before finding the happy fit. There's nothing shameful about this. The shameful thing is to feel miserable about a job— and not try to make it better or find another one.

If you're feeling bored with life, the people around you will be falling asleep as well. If you're sarcastic and antagonistic, they will be too. If you're lukewarm, they will never boil.

So be enthusiastic. Watch the impact that has on the people around you, They'll grow more productive and eager to follow you. Passions, remember, are more powerful than cold ideas. And genuine enthusiasm is contagious.

NEVER UNDERESTIMATE THE POWER OF ENTHUSIASM.

□

Conclusion

MAKING IT HAPPEN

> *Dealing with people is probably the biggest problem you face, especially if you are in business. Yes, and that is also true if you are a housewife, architect, or engineer. Research done under the auspices of the Carnegie Foundation for the Advancement of Teaching uncovered a most important and significant fact—a fact later confirmed by additional studies made at the Carnegie Institute of Technology. These investigations revealed that even in such technical lines as engineering, about 15 percent of one's financial success is due to one's technical knowledge and about85 percent is due to skill in human engineering—to personality and the ability to lead people.*
>
> —**DALE CARNEGIE**

Look out the window. Notice how much change has occurred out there in just the past few years.

The postwar boom went bust. Competition became global. Consumers grew more sophisticated. Quality became an expectation. Whole new industries were born, and others were realigned. Some dried up and blew away. The idea of two military superpowers now seems like ancient history.

The Eastern Bloc fell apart. Europe is growing more unified by the day. The Third World countries are trying to elbow their way onto the economic stage. Most of the cushiness has gone out of modern capitalism—and with it the blessed stability that generations of business people had come to expect.

Did Dale Carnegie anticipate every one of these changes? Of course not. No one could have in a world changing so fast.

But Carnegie did something even more important. He left behind a timeless set of human-relations principles that are just as relevant today as they ever were. And as things turned out, they are uniquely suited to the current high-stress, fast-moving, uncertain world.

Look at things from the other person's perspective.

Offer genuine appreciation and praise.

Harness the mighty power of enthusiasm.

Respect the dignity of others.

Don't be overly critical.

Give people a good reputation to live up to.

Keep a sense of fun and balance in your life.

Three generations of students and business people have benefited from this essential wisdom. More people are benefiting every day.

The timelessness of Carnegie's principles should come as no surprise. They were never rooted in the realities of any particular moment, realities that are guaranteed to change and change. Carnegie tested his principles too long and hard for that. Fads would come and go over the years. Stocks would rise and fall. Technology would accelerate ahead. Political parties would win and lose. And the economic pendulum would swing like a hypnotist's watch—good times, bad times, good times, bad times...

But Carnegie's insights were solid. They merely needed to be applied. They were built around basic facts of human nature, so their essential truth never waned. They worked when the world was humming along. In this new era of constant change, they work just as well. Only now the need for Carnegie's principles—for anything that works —is greater than it's ever been.

So apply these basic lessons and techniques. Make them part of your daily life. Use them with your friends, family, and colleagues. See what a difference they can make.

The Carnegie principles don't require an advanced degree in human psychology. They don't call for years of reflection and thought. All they take is practice, energy, and a real desire to get along better in the world.

"The rules we have set down here are not mere theories or guesswork," Dale Carnegie said about the principles he spent his life teaching to millions. "They work like magic. Incredible as it sounds, I have seen the application of these principles literally revolutionize the lives of many people."

So take those words to heart, and find the leader in you.

□□□